GW00939158

ROGUE HERCULE

With a full load and a cargo of 40,000 lbs,
'Juliet Mike Oscar' will take-off this morning
with an overall weight of 190,000 lbs.
She is, sadly for a veteran, illegal in every sense.
She is improperly certified. She carries an
outrageously unlawful weight. Her flight plan,
which will be filed shortly at air traffic control, is
entirely spurious.
Her cargo is illicit.
Her destination is criminal.

**Also by the same author,
and available in Coronet Books:**

Target Manhattan

Rogue Hercules

Denis Pitts

CORONET BOOKS
Hodder and Stoughton

For Adrienne

Copyright © 1977 by Wyvern Authors (Jersey) Ltd.

First published in Great Britain
by Hodder and Stoughton Limited 1977

Coronet Edition 1979

Printed and bound in Great Britain for
Hodder and Stoughton Paperbacks, a
division of Hodder and Stoughton Ltd.,
Mill Road, Dunton Green, Sevenoaks,
Kent (Editorial Office: 47 Bedford
Square, London, WC1 3DP) by
William Collins Sons & Co Ltd, Glasgow

ISBN 0 340 23469 5

Author's note

The trouble about writing a topical book is that the headlines beat you all the way. Place names change — those in Mozambique will have to stay the way they were when I started — and it's a reasonable bet that Rhodesia won't be Rhodesia any more come publication.

I've taken a lot of liberties with the language of the air for reasons of shorthand. I'm most grateful to RAF, Lyneham for their help and to my friendly neighbourhood arms dealer for his counsel.

Thanks to Mary Livie-Noble who typed tirelessly and to Maureen Rissik and Amanda Hamblin at Hodders for their forbearance.

Denis Pitts,
Wiltshire and Jersey.

FROM THE AIR-CONDITIONED passenger lounge in the ornately new terminal at Karachi International Airport, it is almost impossible to see the small groups of hangars which stand in the extreme north-west quadrant of the airfield complex, a mile from the end of the main runway. They form a sad, neglected set of buildings which had once been painted green and khaki air force camouflage. The paint has faded now, worn by time and sun to an uneven, mottled red.

Most major airports have such an area. This one is guarded by day and night. Those leaving it are searched methodically.

This particular set of corrugated iron buildings is surrounded by a twelve-foot fence of barbed wire. A small sign, placed discreetly so that no airline passenger can be alarmed, says: DANGEROUS CARGO.

One aircraft completely fills the biggest of these hangars. She is fully loaded with fuel and cargo and she sits heavily on her squat, sturdy undercarriage. It is nearly dawn and shortly she will be brought to life.

She is 97 feet long and the span of her high wings is 132 feet. She was built by Lockheed in Atlanta, Georgia, for the US Air Force at a cost of twelve million dollars and she has recently been bought as war-surplus for six million dollars. Her military markings have been removed and she has been sprayed an even shade of matt finish mud brown.

Unlike her scheduled cousins who are lined up by the distant terminals, there is nothing sleek or beautiful about this aircraft. She was built as a tactical troop and freight

7

transport and she is fat and ungainly with a black, bulbous nose and with two equally ugly fuel tanks drooping from her wings. But even here, under the harsh hangar neon strip lighting, you can see that she is brutally tough and functional, with talents not possessed by her commercial neighbours.

Her makers named her Hercules.

She is, in fact, a C 130 H (uprated from the F model by the addition of various avionics). She is powered by four Allison T 56-A7 turboprops, each of them capable of producing 4,050 engine horse power which would be sufficient to raise a Saturn rocket. Her Fairchild radios are VHF and ultra short wave. She houses a V-Cat radar in her nose. The maker's serial number, stamped on a plastic disc on her airframe, is L-382F-100-20.

There are more than a thousand such aircraft flying with various air forces in the West.

The nearest that this one comes to individuality is her radio call sign which is 'Juliet Mike Oscar'.

She is a veteran, a sky-mule, who has been kicked and cursed and rarely loved by her drivers; who has survived tropical storms, electrical storms, powerful updraughts and downdraughts, drunken captains and worthless engineers; who has freighted spent-out combat soldiers from Saigon to Honolulu to return with a consignment of condoms to Bangkok.

She has risen under fire, almost vertically, from short jungle airstrips with a load of desperately wounded men, flying low like a fighter to dodge the Vietcong missiles. She has cracked her undercarriage under the weight of ill-gotten gold bars which a corrupt politician was taking from Vietnam.

She ended her air force career with compassionate distinction by ferrying two hundred orphans to Hong Kong. Then she was laid up, her engines shrouded in polyester sheeting, and stood in an aircraft park in the base at Guam.

There are gashes, badly painted over, in the cabin soundproofing where shell fragments sliced through her during bombardments at Da Nang. She smells of constant use, of men.

Most aircraft have their quirks. Some want to steer left; others vibrate violently at a certain speed and altitude; some are incapable of landing gently; and others are so aerodynamically perfect that even the most hamfisted pilot cannot pancake them.

Juliet Mike Oscar has no such vices. Her logbooks show her to be an exemplary, well-behaved aircraft with no flight eccentricities worth noting.

You enter her from the port side. There are three steps up to the flight-deck which is large and capacious, the ample light tinted gold by the yellow side panels. Her control columns are grimy and stained black with the encrusted dirt from the hands of a thousand pilots and co-pilots. The perspex over the instruments has bloomed at the edges, making some of them difficult to read.

Constant use of the engine condition levers and throttles has worn their plastic coverings away to reveal polished bare metal. A strip of dymotape over the ratio climb and descent meter on the co-pilot's side declares BANG THIS BASTARD HARD AND BE SURE, and the altimeter on the navigator's panel has a similar strip which states: BE WISE, ITS YOUR BALLS. ADD 100 FEET.

The canvas seat covers have frayed, exposing foam rubber bulges; and the seat harnesses have been used so often that they could not possibly be expected to stop a 180 pound man at five times the weight of gravity from hurtling into the windshield.

But she will fly.

She has recently been registered in Spain under fabricated documents. Her four engines were due for a change 140 flying hours ago. Her airframe should have been thoroughly inspected and overhauled, according to the laws of the air, some 500 hours ago.

The Certificate of Airworthiness, secured at present in the captain's brief case, was granted only on the basis of a forged US part 191 certificate under which she had allegedly been maintained.

She will fly. But she will fly illegally.

She is technically in a 'dangerous condition'. She would possibly have been allowed to fly on a very temporary certificate which would lay down stringent conditions in terms of minimum weight and fuel.

The stated overload take-off weight allowed in the maker's specifications for the H model is 175,000 lbs.

With a full fuel load and a cargo of 40,000 lbs, 'Juliet Mike Oscar' will take-off this morning with an overall weight of 190,000 lbs.

She is, sadly for such a veteran, illegal in every sense. She is improperly certified. She carries an outrageously unlawful weight. Her flight plan, which will be filed shortly at air traffic control, is entirely spurious.

Her cargo is illicit.

Her destination is criminal.

Book One

By the time he had reached his thirty-sixth birthday, Martin Gore could no longer be described as handsome. He had been handsome, certainly; indeed even now in the harsh strip lighting of that airport cafeteria it was possible to see why a former girlfriend had called him Byronic. His hair had been long and blond then, but now it had greyed in curious streaks. His nose, which had been long and aquiline, had been pushed out of true in two flying accidents. There was a thin scar two inches long along his chin, the result of a serious car crash. It was a strong, determined face but there was a hardness about it which seemed somehow artificial. It was a face which had known pain and fear, certainly, and yet the eyes were intensely alive and filled with humour. They were large eyes, brown and intelligent, constantly alert in that airport setting.

The tenseness was accelerated now by fatigue and the archness of the neon. He sat, wearing a faded tan bush shirt, and scowled at the sourness of airport coffee which had clearly been reheated ten times or more that night. He had flown that questionable aircraft which stood now in the hangar for three days, and he had not slept properly at any of the planned rest points along the route. He was too aware of the volatile nature of the cargo, of the illegality of this flight which placed his whole flying career in jeopardy.

It had not been an easy haul from Taiwan. The Chinese Criminal Investigation Department had sniffed too industriously and had forced them to fly before they were really ready; the French wireless operator, picked up at the last minute, had defected to a Bangkok bawdy-house with his first cash advance; and the flight over the Pamirs had been a savage mixture of updraughts and downdraughts which had meant long stretches at the controls and mind-rending concentration.

Fatigue brought on layer after layer of irritation which he fought to keep back as he listened to his co-pilot and flight engineer.

"Unsafe? I will personally attest to that fact. She is altogether unsafe."

The flight engineer was a small man with a heavy growth of black beard. His name was George Sroka but he had been known for most of his adult life simply as 'Stubbles'.

"How unsafe?" asked the co-pilot, a squat and yet powerfully built black man called Harry Black.

"Unsafe like the booster hydraulic system reservoir is bleeding like it was mugged, the aileron linkage is corroded and creaks like a haunted house in the movies, and you've heard the way she screams on take-off. Like with agony and perturbation."

As a child in the Bronx, Stubbles had been taught by his father, a Polish-born barman, that it was important that he should learn a new word every day. He had done this all his life but he had never quite succeeded in fitting his new words correctly into sentences. But he knew every bolt, washer, bulb and the bearing of an Allison engine, and every duct and spar and wire of the Hercules airframe. He was a brilliant engineer.

"Are you saying that we shouldn't fly any further?" asked Martin.

"If you will recount several conversations which we had in Taiwan, Captain, you will know too goddamn well that we shouldn't have flown at all," said the engineer. "You gave me five days and a parsimonious allowance of dollars with which to get that aged bucket into an airworthy state. I gave you as far as Karachi. Now the guarantee has expired."

The captain looked directly into Stubbles' eyes and saw genuine worry. Flight engineers are a cautious race, often given to over-exaggeration for the sake of safety. He knew Stubbles. The little man was not being over-cautious now.

Martin turned to Harry who merely shrugged his shoulders.

"All the instruments are registering properly," declared Martin almost defensively.

"Captain, I hear things in those engines that you don't hear either of you." Stubbles voice was normally high-pitched. Now it squeaked.

Martin thumbed through the flight documents on the table in front of him.

"Will we make Cyprus?" he demanded sharply.

Stubbles sighed heavily.

"I guess we can," he murmured. "But I have to tell you the truth, don't I?"

Martin sat very still and placed his two index fingers on either side of his nose. The other two watched him intently. They could see that he was struggling in his mind against the natural airman's reserve which normally dictated their flying.

They were a strange combination, this crew. Martin was English and patrician, Harry was languid, a Texan, and Stubbles was ever alert and querulous like a sparrow. They neither appeared to fit easily together nor, as a crew, did they have any recognisable place among their easily cate-gorised flying brethren.

They were part of the *demi-monde* of the air, contract men, freelancers, mercenaries indeed, respected by scheduled flyers for their ability to fly, but shunned on the ground because they seemed to earn too much money and spend it freely.

They in turn had an equally contemptuous distaste for the flyers with gold bands on their arms who flew to rigid rules, who drank ostentatious orange juices in front of passengers and who demanded precedence at meteorological counters and the other airport offices.

Martin had closed his eyes while he thought. For a few moments the other two watched him closely and wondered if he had fallen asleep.

Then he looked directly at Stubbles.

"We're going to Cyprus," he said in clipped tones. "There's money waiting for us in Cyprus. Are you coming?"

"You bet, Captain," said Stubbles looking around the cafeteria. "I'd hate for to be left in this mausoleum."

They were about to order more coffee when Martin looked up and saw the girl coming towards them.

* * *

She walked across the airport concourse with an easy, athletic stride, a slender girl of mid height with a healthy tan and no make-up, her blonde hair clipped short, her wide, blue eyes alert and intelligent. She showed no sign that she had been travelling since noon the previous day in a complicated series of changes between Brussels and Pakistan.

This was the only time that the normally hectic Karachi airport was quiet during the twenty-four hour cycle. An old Pakistani dozed fitfully behind the giant silver coffee stall; two women, match-thin in their drab grey saris, dragged wet cloths over the cigarette strewn marble floor; even the gaudy souvenir shops were closed. Soon the building would wake again, however, for dawn arrives early in Pakistan and pilots prefer dawn for take-off in those hotter latitudes.

Already there were two or three slip-crews gathering. They sat, paper pale and yawning in the restaurant area, some coughing on their first cigarettes of the day, some wincing, like Martin, at the reheated coffee.

Years of experience could not accustom them to this time of waiting. They talked little. Some read gaudy-covered paperbacks. Others glanced idly at the stewardesses' legs and wrestled with unformed fantasies or fast-fading memories.

Most of the men, however, preferred to follow the blonde girl appreciatively with their eyes as she crossed the hall. The stewardesses, trained to walk with clip-clop uniformity, en-

16

vied the ease of her movements and the simplicity of her blue bush shirt and slacks. A bright red kerchief was tucked into her shirt.

She carried an airline overnight bag which was slung casually over her shoulder. There was a slim document case under her arm.

The name of this girl was Sorrel Francis. She was twenty-four years old, the youngest daughter of a Barberton, Ohio mining family. At the age of sixteen she had been a beauty queen, and when she was eighteen she had worked her way through university in New York as a part-time call girl. Now she was the secretary and the mistress of the man responsible for the arms that were being shipped in Juliet Mike Oscar.

"There's been a change of plans," she said directly. "I'm glad I got here in time or you would have had a two-thousand-mile unnecessary journey."

"You knew we weren't due to leave until the morning," said Martin. "What's happened?"

"These arms are not going to Cyprus," she said. "We don't think they can pay for them."

"Great," said Harry. "What the hell sort of organisation are we working for? An out-of-date chicken coup of an aircraft which scares me rigid on every take-off — and now a change of plan. Where do we go now, back to China?"

"Rhodesia."

Harry blinked several times.

"You're kidding," he said softly.

"We have a buyer in Rhodesia," said Sorrel. "The goodies in the back of your aeroplane are exactly what he wants."

"That's sort of illegal," said Harry. "There's an international embargo on selling knickers to Rhodesia, let alone missiles and mortars."

Martin said nothing. He looked at the girl evenly. She continued.

"Your bonus if this load had got to Cyprus would have been fifty thousand dollars. If you can get it to Salisbury, Rhodesia, within the next forty-eight hours, your bonus will be one hundred and fifty thousand dollars."

The girl looked at the men, awaiting a reaction. It came from Martin.

"Just a few observations," he said. "Firstly, Rhodesia is a long, long way away. We need to consider whether we can make Rhodesia in this aeroplane. Secondly, like Harry says, the world doesn't like Rhodesia which means that we cannot stop over on the way should we need to repair any one of twelve thousand component parts which might go wrong, and probably will, along the route."

Harry said quickly, "We could make it all right. A lot of Hercs make it. Right down the coast of Africa and slide in low over Mozambique. It's only two hundred miles. They've got no radar, no air force, except for a handful of MIG trainers that they can't fly. It's a milk run. It happens all the time."

"That's what Murphy said in Brussels," said Sorrel.

"Did he?" said Martin. "Your boss doesn't have to fly that garbage can out there. He also appears to have failed to take into account the fact that Rhodesia is dominated by a white minority and that Harry is a black man. He might have some sensitivity in that direction."

"Murphy thought on that, too," said the girl. She reached into her document bag. "I'm authorised to pay you off, Harry. Ten thousand dollars in cash."

"And who will co-pilot — even if Harry did take the money?" said Martin harshly.

"Surely there are plenty of out-of-work flyers around here," said Sorrel.

"I suppose that's what Murphy said."

"Something like that."

"Christ, the man's a shit. Of course we can't get anyone else. We're under-crewed as it is."

Harry said quite briskly, "Listen, I don't mind going to Rhodesia or anywhere else if the money's good. I'm no black lover."

Martin looked hard at Sorrel. "All right then," he said. "Supposing Stubbles here agrees to declare the aircraft safe to Rhodesia and supposing I agree to fly it. How sure can we be of the money? It's a shaky, altogether hairy kind of proposition that Mr Murphy's making. How sure can we be of getting paid?"

The girl was getting angry.

"Entirely. I saw the telex messages today. The money has been paid into a bank and will be released on receipt of a coded message from Rhodesia. I know the message. It will be confirmed when you get to Salisbury. You will be paid in cash."

"There?"

"On receipt of the arms, I said that." Sorrel tapped the document case. "The papers are in here. You can see for yourself."

"Why is Murphy so sure that we'll fly?"

"Because I know that all three of you need the money, you in particular. Am I right?"

Martin said, "We've been working for your organisation for three weeks, honey." He was becoming increasingly bitter in the way he spoke. "I will tell you right now that none of us is particularly impressed with the way it works. For one thing we haven't the slightest idea — except for some shrewd perception on all our parts — just exactly who the boss, the real boss, happens to be. There's too much money flying about. I'm prepared to put this to my crew only if I can have some kind of surety that the money will be there. The surety I'm looking for is you."

"No way," she said. "I'm here to give you instructions. I'm not here to risk my life."

Harry looked up from the table.

"The Captain's right. I ain't going unless we've got your sweet little ass as a hostage. And *I'm* superstitious about women on the flight deck."

Stubbles said, "That seems entirely proper to me, too."

The girl looked round at the three men with an expression of defiance and contempt.

"Oh, shit," she said coldly, with exasperation. "I'll come. It looks as though I've got to. Any other conditions?"

Martin toyed for a few moments with a cigarette packet which the girl had left on the table. Finally he extracted a cigarette and lit it with her gold lighter. He inhaled deeply and blew the smoke into the air.

"I'll go if the others will come."

Stubbles said, "For that kind of inducement, I reckon that aircraft is safe."

Harry had been making rough calculations on the plastic table top.

"We'll need to take a good look at the charts," he said. "But I dunno, I reckon we can make it."

"Okay, then we fly," said Martin.

"The only problem is that we've already filed a flight-plan for Cyprus."

"We could stick to it."

"What do you mean?"

Harry said, "We take-off as indicated, hold the course till we've cleared Karachi radar and then sort of turn left."

"Just like that?" asked Martin.

"Just like that."

*   *   *

The Pakistani air traffic controller had clearly been well trained. He marshalled the heavy early morning traffic in a measured, baritone voice. He cleared a Qantas 747 for a quick take-off for London which left a gap of one minute exactly for a BOAC 707 to land from Singapore. The controller passed the Australian captain to radar control and gave ground directions to the crisp voice of the British captain.

He released a Pakistan International Airways internal flight from its holding area on to the main runway.

Martin's voice joined the chatter.

"Good morning Karachi control. Juliet Mike Oscar,

ground checks completed. Permission to taxi, please."

"Juliet Mike Oscar, wait. Pan Am zero zero two you are on finals, wind six knots at one one zero. You are clear to land. Good morning Juliet Mike Oscar. I have your call sign as unscheduled zero zero four. You are clear to taxi. What is your destination, please?"

"Juliet Mike Oscar. Understand unscheduled zero zero four my call sign. My destination is Larnaca, Cyprus."

"Thank you, Captain. Pan Am zero zero two leave the runway at exit one."

The violent dawn revealed the flashing dot on the controller's airport control radar as a lumbering giant, which trundled noisily through the maze of taxi lanes, her four engines screeching unevenly as the crew tested each propeller blade's angle in turn.

Inside her, on her flight-deck, her captain, co-pilot and engineer ran through the ritual catechism of pre-flight checks.

"Auxiliary hydraulic pumps."

Martin steered the aircraft with his left hand on the nose wheel control and read out his lists from a black book in his right hand. There was a faded green canvas document bag on the floor by his side. The stencilled lettering read Flight Lieutenant Martin Gore, RAF.

"Off."

"Flight instruments."

"Checked."

"Propeller reversing."

"Checked."

"Generators and loads."

"Checked, Captain."

"Checked and prayed for and I'll go on praying."

"Cut out the shit, Stubbles." The captain's voice was icily quiet. "Generators and loads."

"Checked."

"Propeller and engine anti-icing."

"Checked."

"Fuel systems."

"Checked."

"Taxi check complete."

Martin relaxed and slipped the book into his document bag.

"Okay then, children," he said. "I suppose no one looked to see if our belly was scraping the floor? It should be with this weight."

"You did the numbers. They looked okay to me." The co-pilot took the loading graph and scanned it. "Just don't try a tactical take-off, that's all, or the wing'll come right off."

The captain turned to him. "Take her please, Harry," he said, as he put on a bright red cap with a badge which read 'Berkshire Golf Club'. He cleaned a pair of orange-tinted spectacles with a Kleenex tissue. He turned to the engineer who sat on the jump seat behind him and the co-pilot.

"What time did you finish this morning?"

Stubbles was adjusting instruments on the roof panel above him. His size was such that each movement meant that he had to stretch with immense difficulty in his harness.

"Finish?" he shrilled. "I could never finish checking out this bucket. Would you believe the state of some of these circuits? Dust, erosion, corruption and kee-rap."

"But I'll get three green lights on arrival?"

"And four fans all the way there."

The captain put on his glasses and replaced his headset.

"Could you do anything at all with the load, Harry?"

"I managed to move the rear three pallets back by about six inches. It might just help the trim. Overloaded like this, you'll have to expect her to fly like a brick shithouse."

They approached the runway, and the heavy regular thumps sent up through the undercarriage by the gaps in the concrete beneath them began to slow as Martin eased on the handbrake and brought the aircraft to a stop. There was a gleaming white Air France DC 10 ahead of them, its engine heat shimmering and swirling in the air behind it.

Martin locked the brake with one half turn and stretched himself, his long arms reaching up to the engineer's controls above him. The sun had risen quickly and the flight-deck was flooded with daylight. He loosened his harness so that he could turn completely in his chair.

"Miss Francis, is everything in order?"

"The hostage is happy," she said primly.

"Don't be bitchy," said Martin. "It's a long run. You'll get used to us."

"What am I supposed to be, anyway?" she demanded. "Your stewardess or cabaret or what?"

"Harry's going to teach you how to listen to the radio," said Martin. "Once we go off track, people are going to be talking about us all over the Middle East. I want to know what they are saying."

Martin glanced at the co-pilot. The other man had not acknowledged the girl's presence. He was stiff and frowned heavily. He did not like women on the flight deck, and he did not hide the fact.

They heard the 747 being cleared for its take-off. They watched it move forward and even in their own noisy cabin, their ears muffled by headphones, they could hear the roar of its engines as it turned on to the runway, accelerating even before the captain had lined it up completely.

"Just to be sitting there in first class," said Stubbles. "Five minutes from now and they'll be hitting the Martinis and caviar and getting ready for the movie. What's our movie, miss?"

"I'll give you Al Jolson at thirty thousand feet," said the captain. An edginess had crept into his voice. He drummed his fingers on the control column. "Come on, come on, come on," he murmured. "We need this gas."

He watched as a twin-engined Cessna made a sharp turn into the flight path and landed in front of them. He released the brake and the aircraft slipped forward.

"Captain to crew, take-off checks."

He reached again for the check list book.

"Ground idle."

"Normal."

"Doors and hatches."

"Closed, warning lights out."

"Pressurisation."

"Set."

The controller's voice loomed in their ears.

"Unscheduled zero zero four, you are clear for take-off. Runway zero two four, wind four knots at one one zero. Ground temperature zero three zero degrees. Climb to one thousand feet and steer two eight zero. Thank you unscheduled and goodday."

"Autopilot."

"Off."

"Flaps."

"Set for take-off."

"Flying controls."

"Checked."

"Hydraulic pressures."

They were talking quickly now. The runway was on their right-hand side and the captain used the engines and nose wheel to put the massive bulk of the C 130 on to the threshold lines. He held it there and looked directly out at the runway. The tail of the Cessna was disappearing to the left. He looked around the sky.

"Fuel panel."

"Set."

"Oil cooler flaps."

"Automatic."

"Seats and harnesses."

"Secure."

The captain turned half right. "Your harness, Sorrel?"

"Good and tight, Captain."

"Instruments."

"Checked and set."

"Take-off information."

"Noted."

"Okay, let's roll. Now you can pray, Stubbles.

The co-pilot eased forward the two inboard propeller controls. The two outer propellers remained in 'reverse' posture. They would stay that way for the first hundred yards or so of the take-off roll; such was the power of the Allisons. The

24

whole airframe shuddered and jerked violently.

The aircraft fought to release itself from the clutch of the brakes but he held her back until the last possible moment.

"Karachi control. Unscheduled zero zero four, you are instructed to delay your take-off and return to the airport building."

The captain grimaced and looked at the co-pilot. He took his hand from the prop controls and pointed his finger down the runway. He moved it to his mouth. The co-pilot nodded. It was a futile gesture and they knew it. The controller's voice would be locked in the Fairchild flight recorders stowed in black and orange boxes in the tip of one wing and the tail of the aircraft.

Martin rammed the brake forward and the struggling, screeching transport ambled forward in a sad anti-climax. A child on a tricycle could have overtaken them for those first few yards. But then she began to gather speed. Twenty-four thousand engine horses struggling with one hundred and ninety thousand pounds, walking, trotting, cantering then galloping down the runway which was already distorted by the morning heat haze.

Martin steered her for the first sixty yards of that runway by the nose wheel and then assumed the flight controls from Harry. They were rolling fast now. Already he was easing forward slightly on the control column.

Even at that stage, this ugly ponderous mastodon was trying to lift its dum-dum nose into the air.

"Karachi control. Unscheduled zero zero four. Abort your take-off. This is an official air traffic instruction. Abort. Abort."

"One twenty knots," said the co-pilot. "That bloke's good. Not a hair out of place. One thirty."

"Screw him."

"One forty knots."

"Stay down there, baby. Good girl." Martin was holding the column well forward now. "Stay down, stay down, honeychile. You just ain't ready to spee-red yo' wings."

"One sixty and rotate."

"Karachi control to unscheduled. Do you receive?"

Martin brought the control column gently towards him.

"Vee one."

They felt the vibrations of the runway stop as the engines lifted her into the air.

"Vee two."

"Gear up."

The three wheels slid into their housing with a gentle bump. Now all shuddering stopped as Juliet Mike Oscar became aerodynamically clean.

"Gear up," confirmed Harry.

"Karachi control." Even now the controller was unperturbed. "Unscheduled zero zero four. Turn left and rejoin the circuit and prepare for landing."

"Karachi control, this is unscheduled zero zero four. We are getting an intermittent signal from you which I cannot read."

They could hear in their headsets the excited voices of others in the control tower. The controller's voice again.

"Karachi control. I repeat you are to land immediately."

"Sorry, Karachi, I appear to have a VHF malfunction. Please repeat."

The captain turned to the co-pilot. "He's cool, man, he's cool," he said. He was smiling. They had reached five hundred feet. There was just one small cloud ahead of them and it glinted a vivid orange in the dawn sun.

A new voice joined in, nasal and smug. "Karachi control, this is Lufthansa two three two. Can I assist by relaying your message to unscheduled?"

The captain bared his teeth. "Oh, up your scheduled arse," he said. "Mr Co-pilot, tell that Kraut to shove it."

"Unscheduled zero zero four to Lufthansa two three two. Adolf, we have a full fuel load and a heavy cargo and we have radio problems with the ground. Kindly go play with your bratwurst and leave us alone. Switching to radar control."

"After take-off checks?"

"Ready. Landing gear."

"As required."

"Flaps."

"As required."

"Landing and taxi lamps."

"Off and set."

They heard the radar controller, a new, high-pitched and cheerful voice, giving them a new course and holding them at a thousand feet.

"He can't have heard."

"They must have given up trying."

"We'll stick to the rules now. We don't have to lose our licences."

The main Drigh road and railway line were beneath them. They could see the ominous Tower of Silence upon which the dead were once placed to be eaten by carrion. The Arabian Sea was a dark blue sheen ahead of them.

"Why are they holding us at this height?" There was a black patch of sweat on the captain's back. Harry reached up and turned the VHF tuning dial.

He listened for a few seconds.

"Man, you'll never guess," he said. "They're scrambling MIGs. That's why they're holding us."

Martin reached down for the undercarriage controls. "I'm dropping to zero feet. Do you read me?"

"I read you."

"Going down."

He snatched the undercarriage lever and air brake controls, adjusting the propellers continually to maintain airspeed. The aircraft buffeted violently and fell like an elevator. They all felt their stomachs shoot suddenly upwards. At five hundred feet he pulled the undercarriage up and throttled forward to full propeller power. He banked hard to the left and brought the plane out of its controlled stall. Still losing height, Juliet Mike Oscar shattered the quiet of Karachi racecourse at two hundred feet and hurtled, screaming like a banshee, over the silent suburb of Clifton at one hundred feet.

It was even lower as it dipped over the silvery white beach

27

and thundered over the pond-like sea so close to the water that its slip-stream left a discernible wake.

The co-pilot was the first to speak.

"Holy Cow," he said. "Since when were you converted to fighters?"

The captain was total, absolute concentration. At that height, an eighth of an inch too much on the control column would destroy them all.

He said evenly, "Harry, give me a course to Salisbury."

And then he added softly, "Kill the radios. We are on our own."

* * *

When he reached his thirtieth birthday just four weeks ago James O'Keefe Murphy, the youngest son of an Anglo-Irish family who lived in happy poverty in a Birmingham suburb, had amassed over £100,000 which he contained in several currencies in many bank vaults in Switzerland, Luxembourg, Liechtenstein and West Germany. He would, quite certainly, have been even more wealthy had it not been for his predilection for the youthful and strapping daughters of clients who were more wealthy than he.

Murphy was of even height, with russet brown hair and a face which even his fellow men acknowledged to be ruggedly attractive. He was a man who glowed with good health and success. His movement was graceful and athletic, his clothes were cut to a conservative perfection by Florentine and Savile Row tailors. He kept a white Rolls Corniche at his villa in Menton and a black, chauffeur-driven Camargue in Brussels. He flew his own private aircraft, a Cessna 390.

Murphy had an almost hypnotic charm which lay behind a shy, angelic smile. He talked softly in a Dublin accent. His proudest boast was that even Gucci assistants were polite to him.

He had a fast intelligence and a pleasing, self-effacing wit. He was, indeed, a vibrant, immensely likeable young man, an ideal weekend guest, the most desirable of all the eligible bachelors in European society.

He was also totally corrupt and ruthless to the point at which human life, unless it was worth money, social advancement or sexual pleasure, was meaningless to him. He had killed frequently, especially during the two years he spent as a mercenary, and he made his fortune by buying and selling other mercenaries to African and Arab states, caring nothing for the causes for which they were supposed to fight, caring even less about their welfare or eventual destiny.

Murphy was the provider.

He sold gelignite to the IRA and Browning machine pistols to the UDA. He treated both with a cheerful impartiality and arranged the freighting and delivery with precision, but always on strictly cash terms. He could provide heavy and light tanks, missiles, howitzers, fighters, bombers and helicopter gun-ships. He had an option at this moment to sell two cruisers and a flotilla of destroyers. They were worth to him one per cent of one per cent of twelve million dollars.

It was before dawn now and Murphy was driving at one hundred and twenty miles per hour along the autostrada from Rome to the outskirts of Naples.

The quadruphonic stereo-deck was playing discreet jazz. Murphy was holding a white telephone in one hand, talking rapidly. There was a beautiful dark-haired girl beside him and she slept happily in the reclining seat.

*   *   *

The news of the disappearance of Juliet Mike Oscar from the Karachi radar screens was passed within a few minutes to the duty officer at the Ministry of Foreign Affairs in Moscow by the Air Attaché at the Soviet Embassy, who had been monitoring the VHF frequencies at Karachi Airport.

The Ministry, in turn, relayed the message to the one person in Moscow who had been maintaining a constant trace of the C 130 from its starting point in Taiwan, through Bangkok, and across Bangladesh, Nepal, Northern India, into Pakistani air space. It was 4.00 am, Moscow time.

The woman who took the telephone call had been dancing and she was slightly breathless as she spoke to the duty officer. He, in turn, frowned slightly at the idea of a senior government official being in a nightclub at that hour in the morning. He had to shout over the sound of rock music which blared in the background.

"Good morning, Comrade Rogov," he said. "I have further news for you. Your assumption was entirely correct."

"One moment." The duty officer heard her ordering an obvious drunk away from the telephone. "Go on," she said.

"The target aircraft has turned south at Karachi and is obviously not flying to Cyprus."

"As I anticipated. Its course?"

"It has eluded radar surveillance."

There was a silence from the other end of the line. The duty officer, who was close to retirement, said, "Comrade, are you there?"

"I am thinking."

A Beatles record was playing now. The duty officer continued to frown. Then the woman's voice came on again. She was brisk and businesslike now.

"Please inform Comrade Minister Gromyko and Comrade Marshal Levkov as soon as they are awake. I shall be at my desk in thirty minutes and will require a full transcript of the Karachi report."

"Very good, Comrade."

He heard the telephone click down and pushed a buzzer on his desk for a messenger.

The duty officer was a communist of the old school, a survivor of various regimes who would soon accept his state pension and retire to his home village in the Urals. He disliked jazz music and young women like this one. The revolution, he decided, was a long way from succeeding.

Thirty minutes after the duty officer in Moscow replaced his telephone receiver another telephone call was being taken, this time six thousand miles away in a large and tastefully furnished apartment which overlooked Central Park South in New York City. Three men sat around the dining table in this room drinking brandy. It was nearly midnight but the streets outside were noisy and the double-glazed windows vibrated from the throb of traffic.

It was the eldest of these men who took the telephone call. He was tall and thin with a gaunt, cadaverous face which was enlivened only by large, intelligent brown eyes which flashed continually around the room as he listened to the caller, speaking only when he needed something repeated.

His companions at the table were considerably smaller than he was. One had horn-rimmed glasses and fat, reddening jowls with thick, ugly lips. The other was of middle height with greying hair which appeared to be heavily brilliantined, and a razor-thin moustache which was jet black and ludicrous.

All three men were criminals. They were exceedingly powerful criminals. They were made all the more powerful because they had achieved the level of respectability in society which is brought by absolute wealth, by the shrewd investment of that wealth, and by the creation around them of legends, most of which are totally apocryphal. They delighted in being called leaders of the *Mafiosa*; they could afford to do so because they also basked in the knowledge that they were above the law.

The name of the man who took the telephone call was Pietro Ragnelli. He was sixty-five years old and he was a millionaire several times over from the proceeds of prostitution and extortion but mainly, like his two colleagues, from the illegal importation and sale of addictive drugs.

He had been in his time a considerable hoodlum and bully. But of recent years, particularly since the acquisition of vast sums of cash and with his elevation to near film star status by the press and television networks, he had cultivated a pose of quiet, thoughtful affability. He had spent several thousand dollars, for instance, on speech therapy to replace the rasping accent of Hells Kitchen with a curious, toneless, mid-American accent which was more menacing.

He waited for a few minutes before speaking. His eyes were closed and he drummed his fingers on the edge of the table.

"Well now, gentlemen," he said very quietly. "It is fortunate that you are here. I am sorry that I have to use a social occasion for such a purpose, but I am afraid that at least one person has to die in the next few hours and, as you will recall, we have covenanted together not to put out any contracts except by mutual agreement."

The others watched him. Their expressions did not change.

"This death, or these deaths, will take place out of the territory of the United States which may make what I am going to say somewhat superfluous in terms of our agreement. However, one of them is certain to take place on Italian soil and this, I believe, is within the spirit of the agreement."

The two men nodded quietly.

"I will explain," said Ragnelli. "As you know, I have invested substantial sums of money in the purchase of war-surplus aircraft and weapons through completely legal nominee companies in the Bahamas, Nicaragua, Luxembourg, and Liechtenstein. This has been a profitable investment and it has the unspoken approval of the State Department, the Department of Defence and the United States Treasury, all three of whom have gained in one way or another from these transactions.

"Unfortunately, this good relationship has now been jeopardised by the action of one man. Let me explain further. It has been a basic policy of my operation that the surplus weapons are sold strictly according to International Law. In other words, gun-running is not allowed, no matter what the temptation.

"Two years ago I appointed as an agent a young man named James Murphy. He has handled much of my European operation with great flair and success and has done well financially from his work."

Ragnelli placed his finger-tips on the table in front of him.

"Murphy has now decided to break the rules and put me at risk. Using a position of trust and using my contacts, Murphy has managed to steal one of my aircraft, to fill it with weapons and to arrange for it to fly with those weapons to Rhodesia which is, as you know, the subject of a strict international arms embargo."

He paused. For a moment he was playing the Supreme Court judge.

"It will not be easy, gentlemen, for me to explain this to those in authority. In the past twenty-four hours I have tried to stop the flight of this aircraft at various points along its route. Tragically, my representative arrived too late in Pakistan to stop it from taking off from Karachi. My assumption is that Murphy is in radio contact with this aircraft and the immediate task is to persuade him to divert it to any country except Rhodesia. Thereafter, with your approval, Murphy will die and so, I fear, will the crew of the aircraft." Ragnelli slammed his hands on the table. His colleagues said nothing, just looked at him.

"It is important that others should not be led into such misguided behaviour," he said. "I take it I have your approval?"

"It's okay with me," said the horn-rims. He poured a brandy. "Mind you, I always said you should put your money into movies."

"Go on ahead," said the second one.

"Thank you," said Ragnelli. "I am fortunate that one of my very best operatives is in Naples at this very moment. And so is Murphy."

*   *   *

The sea was no longer a mill-pond. There were waves now, and whitecaps. A strong crosswind had forced the captain to climb to one hundred feet and, even at that height, he needed all his skill to hold the aircraft in level flight. The wind was uneven and capricious and tried all the time to tip Juliet Mike Oscar on to her side.

"Fifteen minutes from the shoreline, Captain. We should be clear of their radar now." Sweat was streaming down Harry Black's face. He found it impossible not to hide the fear and excitement of the sea-level gamble.

"Look around for any stray aircraft."

The co-pilot loosened his harness and clutched at a hand-grip and he looked through the side panelling.

"Clear to starboard," he said.

Stubbles shouted, "Nothing on my side."

"No vapour lines?"

"Nothing. Not many people fly this way."

"Okay then, I'll climb. Give me ten degrees of flap. I'll take it slowly. I'd hate for them to see us now."

Slowly, awkwardly, the giant aircraft lifted herself from the sea and made towards a bank of clouds on the horizon.

As they reached a thousand feet, the captain said, "Your controls." Harry's hands slid out automatically and took the control column. They were on top of the surface wind now and she flew easily and steadily.

The captain took off his golf cap and sunglasses and shook himself in his seat. He took a small hand towel from the bag at his side and wiped the sweat from his face.

"Some bastard whispered real loud back there. Sod him. Stubbles, tell me what that imitation of a speedboat did for our fuel reserves."

The engineer held a slide rule in one hand and wrote a series of figures on a notepad on his knee. "Any moment now, Captain, and Einstein will announce his theorem. You have a fifteen minute reserve at destination which means that you have lost three per cent of your five per cent allowance which is what I would say was cutting things very fine."

"For TWA maybe," said Harry.

"For unscheduled zero zero four, likewise."

Martin said thoughtfully, "An airframe which is carrying twenty million dollars' worth of high explosive shit to the white man in Rhodesia is hardly likely to find a friendly face in any of the countries between here and there."

"Even for one of their American cousins?" said Harry. "My visa is written all over my face."

"I don't fancy one of your African cousins putting me and Stubbles in a bloody great stewpot," Martin grunted. He held up a chart. "Somalia, that's one place we've got to avoid at all costs. They cut your balls off in Somalia."

"And fry them in a skillet while you wait," Harry interjected ominously.

"You mean, like in Sardis? Always wanted to go to Sardis," shouted Stubbles.

"Kenya, Tanzania, Mozambique."

"Not a friendly filling station for miles."

"So we go all the way there and hope to Jesus that the weather stays clean and we don't meet any real headwind. And may I remind you just once more that there's a gold pot at the end of the rainbow."

The co-pilot muttered into his mouthpiece. "I sure enough hope so because we've lost our flying licences, that's for sure."

The captain loosened his harness and stood up. He unplugged his intercom and walked to the rear of the flight deck. The girl was nervous but smiled bravely.

He plugged his intercom into a bulkhead jack and stroked her head.

"How are you feeling?" he asked. The chill, professional voice had disappeared.

"After that flight I feel drained. I didn't know you could fly so low."

"Wait until we get to Mozambique. We'll be so low under their radar that I'll reach out and pick you orchids."

"Don't bother."

"Is there a Coke in the ice-box?"

"I'll get you one."

"No, stay there. She's still liable to bounce a little."

35

Martin climbed down the steps from the flight-deck and opened the small refrigerator. He took a can of Coca-Cola from it and pulled sharply on the ring.

At that precise moment there was a loud 'crack' from the port wing behind him. The aircraft yawed suddenly. A great gush of oily black smoke was pouring from the starboard outer engine.

*　　　*　　　*

The African Affairs Department of the Vladimir Ilyich Lenin Institute for Foreign Studies occupied three entire floors of a gaunt, granite building in the campus of Moscow University. It had a staff of three hundred men and women, many of them African graduates of the Patrice Lumumba 'Friendship' University.

The head of this department was a woman of middle height with striking auburn hair and a face of considerable beauty. Her name was Natalia Rogov. She was thirty-five years old. She had brown eyes which were slightly slanted but only vaguely oriental, and cheekbones which were high yet not so high as those of her Mongolian forefathers; her nose was slim and slightly upturned and her mouth was generous.

Natalia Rogov was a complete anachronism in the bureaucratic hive in which she worked for fourteen hours of each day. Her soft tan suede suit was tailored by Cardin, her cosmetics were Elizabeth Arden, her hand-made shoes from Rayne.

She belonged, in appearance indeed, to the lobby of Claridges or to an apartment block on East 57th Street in Manhattan. Her body was slender and her movements supple, her breasts were ample and firm, and she preferred not to fasten the two top buttons of the silk shirts which she favoured.

She was extremely feminine and sexually magnetic. She

was an outstanding example of the newly emancipated Russian woman.

Stalin would have had her tried and probably shot as a deviationist whore, and the prudish Krushchev would have branded her as a painted Western revisionist and made her wear black serge and lisle stockings. The present government, while frowning heavily upon those decadent western tastes and her leggy, disturbing presence at Central Committee meetings, had allowed her the maximum freedom because she had the one attribute which they crave in their young, success.

Apart from being politically brilliant and diplomatically astute, Natalia Rogov was one of the prime architects of Soviet policy in Southern Africa.

The Lenin Institute was a unique establishment with an unusual amount of autonomy. It was manned, throughout the twenty-four hours of each day, by teams of leading academicians and intellectuals whose task it was to make decisions affecting the future of the Marxist-Leninist philosophy throughout the world. Some were concerned with five, ten, fifty years ahead. Others were making instant decisions and recommendations on ways of taking advantage of weaknesses in the western system.

On this particular morning, as the crew of Juliet Mike Oscar fought to kill a deadly fire three thousand feet over the Arabian Sea, Natalia Rogov had walked alone to her office through the grey first light. The aircraft was paramount in her mind, except that she saw it abstractly as a particularly critical pawn in her personal African chess game.

While Moscow slept, she sat at her desk and talked into a dictaphone for more than an hour. She began with a thorough analysis of Russian policy in Southern Africa and outlined its various successes. She dealt with United States policy in equal depth.

"It has become abundantly clear that some urgent action must be taken to discred........................ role being played by imperialist governments in regard to Rhodesia," she said.

"The aircraft to which I have referred at the commencement of this report provides an excellent opportunity.

"It is an American aircraft which has been used in Vietnam. It is owned by a company which is owned by Pietro Ragnelli who is a leading name in organised crime in the United States. Ragnelli is a close friend of influential United States politicians. (See photographs, Appendix C.) And it is flown by two Americans and a Briton.

"The aircraft is carrying a large quantity of missiles ground-to-air, air-to-ground, anti-tank, together with anti-personnel bombs, heat-detonated mines and other anti-guerrilla weapons."

Natalia Rogov paused and lit a black cigarette. She looked at a picture of the aircraft which had been taken the previous day in Bangkok.

"It is my recommendation that action be taken which will cause the maximum embarrassment to the United States Government. My assumption is that this aircraft will deliberately and illegally overfly Mozambique. I recommend that the aircraft be brought down, preferably relatively unharmed, over Mozambique territory and that the crew and the cargo should be placed on display to the press and media of the world, thus incriminating those criminals who have encouraged this flight, namely the President and the Defence Department of the United States."

Natalia Rogov played back the last few minutes of her dictation. She picked up the microphone. She said, "Please mark this 'OF EXTREME URGENCY' and have it ready, five copies only, for nine o'clock this morning."

*   *   *

The sequence of events which follows immediately after the sounding of a fire warning in a multi-engined aircraft is simple, swift and singularly undramatic. A siren wails and a red light flashes. The first action of the pilot is to engage the

38

mechanism which shuts down the supply of aviation fuel to the engine and floods it with chemical extinguishers.

A well-trained crew will then enter a series of routines, each of them carefully worked out by the manufacturers and operators of the aircraft, to establish the cause of the fire and its immediate effect. Fire in the air is an airman's greatest fear, and yet the seconds or minutes which follow the alarm must be devoid of all panic. The routines are carried out, again from the small black check-list manual which each member of the crew carries.

The talk is low-keyed, monotone. The concentration is absolute.

In the C 130 the warning system is contained in five inverted 'T'-shaped handles which are made of transparent plastic and contain red-coloured lights. Four of these represent engines and the fifth is an alarm for the hydraulic system.

Harry Black was already tugging briskly at the flashing number one 'T' handle as Martin leapt back on to the flight-deck. The alarm siren had already stopped as the captain got into his seat and rammed his intercom jack into its socket.

"Engineer, what's the nature of the fire?"

"Pitch lock, Captain, in number one engine. The RPM went way over limits, turbine inlet temperature rose to eleven hundred degrees."

"Hit the feather button."

"I have. She won't feather."

Martin adjusted the rudder trim to counter the yawing effect on the giant aircraft caused by the sudden loss of power in the port wing. Juliet flew straight and level, but her whole frame was vibrating furiously.

"Hit it again."

From the corner of his eye he saw the tiny engineer lean over to the feather over-ride controls and crash his fist down on the first of them. It immediately flew up again.

The outer port propeller had stopped. It was locked in a fine pitch position which meant that four wide propeller blades were creating a wall of solid drag. The effect was rather like that of streaming a parachute from the port wing tip. The vibration increased, so did the screaming of the engines.

"We're losing height, Captain."

"Thank you, Co-pilot."

"Two hundred feet a minute."

"Thank you." The captain's voice was almost absurdly polite. He looked at his altimeter. It showed 3,000 feet. He said very precisely, "Mr Engineer, you have fifteen minutes to get that propeller turning. We will begin to dump fuel in five minutes."

The little engineer was thumbing through pages of circuitry diagrams. The co-pilot held a chart on his lap and made rapid calculations with a slide rule.

"For your information, Captain, if we lighten the fuel load by one hundred kilos a minute, we could possibly make Oman. Or we could return to Karachi."

"Negative!" Martin almost spat it out. "Hold the present course."

He leaned forward and looked at the outer engine blades. The propeller appeared to be on the point of buckling against the force of the air, but he knew it would hold.

He spoke rapidly. "Miss Francis, I'll explain what is happening. We have an emergency. With our present cargo and fuel load, unless Stubbles can feather number one propeller, we may have to ditch.

"You will find lifejackets under the bunk behind you. Put one on and place one by each member of the crew. Then strap yourself firmly in your seat and wait."

*　　*　　*

Natalia Rogov did not bother to hide her considerable anger as she sat down at the walnut ministry table. She had insisted on an immediate meeting with Andrei Gromyko, the Foreign Minister. Instead, she faced the fat and slow-speaking Stephanovich Tchakev, the Third Deputy Minister for

Foreign Affairs, a man renowned in the Soviet structure for his heavy-handed pedantry and capacity for survival.

"I take it the Comrade Minister has read my report?" she snapped.

"No more than your summation and recommendations, Comrade Rogov."

"And?"

"You realise the extreme seriousness of what you are suggesting?"

It was a typically soulless, functional committee room on the fourth floor of the Soviet Foreign Ministry. The woodwork was brown and the walls, originally washed white, were yellow and faded. Lenin's portrait scowled and Brezhnev's beamed from one wall. And on a blackboard at the end of the room was a map of Africa.

There were five men and one woman around the walnut table. Two of the men were Foreign Ministry officers who said nothing during the meeting but nodded agreement continually with the Third Deputy Minister. The other two were dressed in the smart olive-green uniforms of the Red Air Force. They too said nothing, but made continual notes.

At another table an elderly woman in a black dress, her grey hair swept severely back, sat and made shorthand notes of all that was said. She occasionally looked up to glower over her spectacles at the Head of African Affairs, who wore this morning a tight black sweater and ivory-coloured slacks.

"The danger is obvious, Comrade Rogov. You are recommending that this aircraft should be shot down. How do we know that it may not be on an entirely legitimate journey with an entirely legal cargo? If we, or our allies, molest it in any way, the Soviet Union would be open to the charge of conspiracy to international piracy."

Natalia opened a heavy file on the table in front of her.

"I have ample evidence, Comrade Minister."

"Produce your evidence."

"You realise the extreme urgency of this matter, Comrade Minister?" she said.

The Third Deputy Minister took off his heavy horn-rimmed glasses and polished them with a white handkerchief. "I am a lawyer, Comrade," he said. "I wish to see all the facts before I make any recommendation for any action, no matter how urgent you may think it may be."

"Very well, but I do ask for the maximum speed and decision. Firstly the crew of this aircraft. The captain. His name is Martin Michael Gore, he is aged thirty-six. He is the only son of Sir Peter Gore of Pewsey in Wiltshire. The young Gore was educated at Marlborough College which is a Public School in England and expelled for a series of pranks which led to the burning down of the college gymnasium. He joined the Royal Air Force and became a Hercules pilot at Lyneham in Wiltshire and achieved the rank of Flight Lieutenant before he was cashiered after four years' service for striking a superior officer. For two or three years after this it is known that he was a freelance charter pilot and, as you will see from the attached records, he went to America. There it is believed that he spent some considerable time at the special Services Training Establishment which is a Central Intelligence Agency affiliate at Pompano, Florida. His exact function at that institute is not known but it is generally believed that his particular skills as a low-level pilot were put to use by the CIA. Until six months ago he was the personal pilot of Amin, the President of Uganda."

"So?" The Third Deputy Minister had put his glasses back on and assumed a look of disinterest. He scarcely glanced at the paper which Natalia put in front of him.

"Comrade Minister, Captain Gore is clearly an aristocratic renegade. The CIA connection is important in this matter."

"You have a point."

"The co-pilot," Natalia was speaking rapidly now with little emotion. "Harold Irving Black, aged thirty-five, an American citizen. He was educated privately and then at the University of Texas where he obtained a Bachelor of Science degree with Class One Honours. He was conscripted into the United States Air Force in 1967 and flew seventy-six missions in this type of aircraft. He was wounded three times, awarded the Air Force Cross for Gallantry. His service record, a copy of which is also produced, shows that he spent a year in the same establishment in Florida as Martin Gore. He was Gore's co-pilot with General Amin."

"Continue, Comrade."

"Comrade Minister, the fact is that the co-pilot of this aircraft is a negro."

Tchekov tapped his spectacle case with his finger-tips impatiently.

"There are many negro flyers."

"Comrade Minister, I cannot truly believe that a black pilot would be prepared to fly arms to the white renegade army in Rhodesia, unless ordered to do so."

"You have a point, Comrade."

"The engineer of this aircraft is Madison George Sroka, a second generation Polish-American, also a Vietnam veteran. He was honourably discharged from the US Air Force two years ago. He has been a civilian maintenance man at the Guam airbase until recently."

Tchakev continued to tap his fingers.

"This is interesting, but it is not evidence, Comrade. There is nothing at all to suggest that this aircraft is flying to Rhodesia, nor that it is carrying arms."

Natalia opened a gold cigarette case from her handbag and lit a Benson and Hedges. She noticed that one of the Air Force colonels had his eyes gazing fixedly on her bosom.

"Please let me continue. There is a fourth member of this crew, according to the manifest, a copy of which I received this morning from the agent in Karachi. Her name is Sorrel Francis. She is twenty-four years old, also an American citizen. This woman has, for the past two years, been secretary to James O'Keefe Murphy who is the Managing Director of Interguns Inc of Brussels, which is known to be a nominee company owned by organised crime in the United States. KGB report of January 4th, 1974 shows clearly that this company, while outwardly concerned with the import and export of steel tubes, is ninety per cent concerned with the import and export of illicit arms, mainly from

American War-Surplus supplies in the Far East to African states and other emergent countries. You will have seen my memorandum of this morning concerning the Mafia and its involvement with this company.

"The woman Francis flew from Brussels to Karachi yesterday. It is my belief that the reason for her flight was to instruct the crew to divert the aircraft from its intended journey to Cyprus to Rhodesia. I do not need to remind the Minister of the present situation in Rhodesia. The outlaw Ian Smith and his co-conspirators continue to defy international opinion and face a violent struggle against the freedom fighters of the black countries surrounding them. They are desperate for arms and we have substantial evidence of their dealings with various companies in the West. Interguns is the most unscrupulous of all these arms-dealing companies and you will find attached to this report a number of cables and telex messages between the Ministry of Defence in Salisbury and Interguns offices in Brussels, Monte Carlo and Naples."

There was a long silence in the committee room. Then the Minister spoke.

"I need to be absolutely certain that this aircraft is flying arms, Comrade. You realise the implications of what you are suggesting. You are asking for an aircraft to be brought down, possibly with fatal results. The Soviet Union would face extreme international embarrassment were it to be proved that this aircraft was carrying a consignment of woolly dolls."

Natalia, who now fought desperately hard to avoid showing her total impatience, brought a new edge to her voice as she said, "Minister, if you would care to examine Appendix E of this file which has been on your desk since before 6.00 am this morning, you will see that it is a copy of the cargo manifest of C 130 H JMO which is attached to a copy of the flight plan from Karachi to Cyprus. Would you like me to read it to you? Item. Red-eye missiles (F 2 & 3) complete, Number 180. Fragmentation grenades, 2,000. M 16 1A1 5.6mm rifles, each with two spare magazines, quantity 1,000. Body-heat activated anti-guerrilla mines, 500 . . . Do I need to continue, Comrade Minister? Do they sound like woolly dolls?"

Tchakev put his hand out and took Natalia's cigarette box from the table. He admired it for a moment, then opened it and took out a cigarette.

"English, eh? Anything else, Comrade Rogov?" He lit the cigarette with a spluttering Russian match.

"There was an attempt to stop the aircraft from taking off this morning," she said. "Our agent reports that someone, possibly the CIA, became interested in the fact that we were interested."

Tchakev looked at the papers on the table in front of him.

"Very well, Comrade Rogov, I am sufficiently convinced to speak immediately to Comrade Minister Gromyko. But I must point out that the decision to bring down the U2 spy plane in such a way as to leave it largely undamaged and to save the pilot for international exhibition was taken at the level of the President of the USSR and the General Secretary of the Communist Party. It was also ratified by the Central Committee. You realise the responsibility which you are undertaking?"

"Most certainly, Comrade Minister."

Tchakev stood up, gathered the papers and smiled a watery smile around the table.

Before he could leave the room, however, Natalia stood as well. Her eyes were fierce now, her voice trembling.

"Comrade Minister, I have tried to stress the urgency. This aircraft is already in flight. Unless we act immediately, it may well be that these arms will be used against the People's Armies of Mozambique and Zambia by the illegal forces of the reactionary Smith and his regime in Rhodesia."

Tchakev sighed.

"Comrade Rogov, I admire the passion of your advocacy. I think I must tell you now that I would be grateful if you would remain, all of you, sitting around this table. I shall see the minister with the strongest recommendations that the course of action which you have proposed is implemented immediately. I would be grateful if our comrades from the

Red Air Force would consider how best this aircraft can be brought down leaving the maximum amount of evidence and preferably saving the lives of the crew members in order that they can be put on an international show trial in the very near future."

Natalia glanced at her wristwatch.

It would take an hour at least for Gromyko to make up his mind. Then Brezhnev would have to make the final decision. She looked at Gore's picture on the table. Even in the service identity photograph he was trying to repress a smile.

"I'll make you grin, you bastard," she thought.

*   *   *

Sorrel Francis sat at the Navigator's table in Juliet Mike Oscar and watched the three men fighting at the controls to save the aircraft as it continued its slow but inevitable descent towards the sea beneath them. There, at the back of the flight-deck, encased in a mae-west lifejacket, she could see it all with a curious detachment. For one thing, she marvelled that she was not afraid. The low flying had been almost exhilarating until the sea itself had begun to splash and salt settle on the windshield, and there had been a moment of true terror when the fire alarm had sounded.

But now, listening to the men talk through her earphones and only half understanding the involved technicalities which they muttered, she felt little fear.

Had I been in the back of any scheduled airliner in an emergency, she thought, I would have been terrified near to death by now. I would be clutching on to anything, I'd probably be screaming my head off and wetting my pants.

"2,000 feet, Captain."

"Roger."

She could sense the two pilots willing the giant plane to keep height. There was no sense of strain in Martin's movement, especially in the way he moved the controls, gently, feather-like, back and forth. Earlier on the airport approach, as he was waiting anxiously to take-off, his knuckles had been white and she had seen the muscles tauten on the back of his neck. Now, faced with a real emergency, he was almost relaxed.

"Engineer."

"Captain?"

"You've no way of losing that propeller altogether?"

"Sorry, captain."

She was intrigued by the speed with which the engineer worked. He leapt from side to side on the flight-deck checking instruments on both sides, looking at diagram after diagram in his flight manual and all the while seeming to ignore the colossal shuddering of the aircraft as three good propellers sucked up the air which their fouled neighbour battered with its four two-feet wide blades. At one point he found time to turn to her and wink.

"Captain, we should start to jettison now."

Harry Black held up a chart which he had drawn in a chinagraph pencil on a large piece of plastic which had been divided into graph squares.

"The red line is us," he said. The red line on the plastic dropped directly to the bottom. Martin looked at it.

"You know what you are saying?"

"I've had time to look at the sea, Captain," said Harry. "We'll never ditch. If we lighten the fuel load we can gain height and maybe land in one of the Gulf States at least."

"They'll impound the cargo."

"Don't I know?"

"150,000 bucks, we've lost."

"I have also looked at the Aviators' Almanac. That's a shark-infested sea down there. And looking at the state of these lifejackets I wouldn't give much chance for the dinghy. And one more thing. At least if we gain height we might be able to make short wave contact with the contractors. Perhaps they'll have some sort of idea."

47

They were dropping slowly into low, scudding clouds between which the occasional sudden glimpse of the sea became even more ominous. They were close to the water now and Martin could see that the other pilot was right. The waves had grown in height and the sea was ragged. There were no even troughs into which he might make any kind of landing, even if he could maintain control in that wind with an aircraft in this condition.

"Engineer, stop everything else and get ready to blow fuel," he said. "Co-pilot, how much to take us to 20,000 feet?"

"Call it 50,000 lbs, Captain."

"You heard him, Stubbles. Jettison fuel."

From her seat in the back of the flight-deck, Sorrel watched the small engineer reach up and open a red-lined glass-covered case and flick a series of switches.

At the very tip of each wing a small valve was opened electrically and two powerful hydraulic pumps began to blast air into the main wing-tip fuel tanks, forcing a steady flood of JP1 kerosene into the atmosphere at ten gallons per second. Two great streams of vapour began to widen rapidly behind Juliet Mike Oscar.

Harry Black tapped hard on the climb and descent indicator. He watched the needle. It did not move at first. And then it began to quiver very slightly towards the horizontal line.

"She's flying level."

Sorrel's eyes were on the captain. He was not sweating now. He was at one with the machinery around him, totally calm.

"Five degree angle of climb. Thirty thousand pounds jettisoned. Ten thousand more will give you fifteen degrees, Captain. You will have 20,000 feet in thirty-five minutes, sooner if we get that prop to feather."

The aircraft was climbing very slowly. But she was climbing. No longer could Sorrel see the looming sea and horizon. Very slowly, still hammered by the wind, still juddering and buffeting in her near crippled condition, Juliet Mike Oscar

48

pulled herself through the clouds into the clear air above.

"Fifteen degrees of climb."

"Close fuel vents." .

"All vents closed and secured. Pumps off." *

"Stubbles?"

"Yes, Captain."

"Don't tell me there's not an emergency drill to get that propeller turning. You must have something in that book of yours. And Sorrel?"

"Yes, Captain."

"Somehow we've got to get a message to Interguns. Now I'm going to ask Harry when he's not one hundred per cent busy to punch out a Selcal signal which should get through to Murphy if he's awake. We're going to have to take a chance even if the whole world gets to know. The message is going to read — now write this down — 'Juliet Mike Oscar, one engine dead, propeller locked. Negative intended destination. Negative return Karachi'."

Martin swung the control column gently to the right, holding the aircraft in a steady climb.

" 'My destination now Muscat with ETA' — can you work that out Harry, please — 'please advise urgently.' "

Sorrel was writing quickly on a pad on the table in front of her.

The Selcal system is used by airlines to speak to individual aircraft. It operates by a series of coded pulses, almost like a telephone. Within minutes, Sorrel's clear voice was being beamed to Cairo Radio and thence by short wave to Naples.

*   *   *

It took twenty minutes for a reply to reach Natalia Rogov and the waiting air force officers. It came in a long, buff-coloured envelope and was delivered by a uniformed KGB man.

Natalia opened it. The message contained on the yellow-coloured paper headed 'From the Office of the Supreme

49

Praesidium' was singularly short for a Russian official document. It read:

"Proceed with the operation as outlined in N Rogov's morandum today. The Ministry of Defence and Diplomatic Service and all intelligence units are to give the maximum assistance.

"The maximum propaganda must be made of this American hypocrisy."

Natalia passed the paper to the two air force men. They looked at it briefly and smiled up at her.

"Well, Comrades," she said. "Have you considered how this is going to be done?"

*   *   *

They had pulled themselves fifteen thousand shaking, shuddering feet from near sea level before Stubbles finally found the fault. A small, almost microscopically small piece of metal dust, shaken up by the sudden manoeuvring of the aircraft, had lodged in one vital circuit breaker in the panel of several hundred on his left-hand side. He had pushed each of these in turn and then, finally, almost in complete disgust, he had jabbed painfully at them with his thumb giving each a muttered curse.

The thumb system worked. He looked at the other wall of the fuselage, at the feather-over-ride panel. Suddenly a red light was flashing where there had been no light before. With his finger-tips, he pushed the feathering knob down.

They all felt it happen at once. The unevenness disappeared from the engines and the vibration eased. Martin glanced through his side panel and saw number one propeller turn slowly and then gather speed. Automatically he adjusted his rudder controls to allow for the sudden new freedom. Number one was useless in terms of power, but it was no longer a dangerous hindrance.

There had been little talk on the flight-deck during the gradual climb to safety. For one thing, no one was anxious to distract the engineer or to panic him into making a fatal mistake.

The two pilots had been equally preoccupied as they took five-minute spells alternatively at the controls. The concentration required to maintain a steady climb with this almost impossible power configuration was desperately tiring, especially when they were never far from that speed at which Juliet Mike Oscar could stall and flip onto her back if the pilot was even momentarily diverted.

But now it had eased for all of them. The aircraft was in level, steady flight, her agony finished.

Martin made one final adjustment to the trim and checked the instruments one by one. He snapped on the automatic pilot.

"How did you manage it?" said Martin with relief in his voice.

"Don't ever ask me, Captain," said the engineer. He had taken off his shirt and was rubbing his body down with an oily towel. "Like I told you, this elderly lady, this alleged aeroplane should be in a geriatric ward."

"What caused the fire?"

"A secondary bearing. A blocked oil feed I would guess. Must have been running white hot."

"After that abort signal at Karachi I smell sabotage."

"No way. I warned you that this aircraft is not safe. That engine should have been replaced before the Civil War. Just keep your fingers crossed for the other three. They sound all right to me but anything can happen."

Martin rose from his seat and eased himself down the three steps into the cargo department. He stood in the spot where he had been when the explosion took place. The can of Coca-Cola was on the ledge as he had left it. It was warm now and tasted sweet-and-sour in his mouth. He looked at number one engine. The cowling had blackened, except where the heat had peeled off the paint. Thin streams of black oil oozed from the rivets around the access hatches.

He took three more tins from the ice-box and eased himself back up on to the flight-deck. He handed Cokes to

51

Sorrel and Harry and a Budweiser beer to Stubbles. They each looked at him with curiosity as he plugged in and started to speak.

"Time, it seems, for a status report," he said. "We are in an unhappy status. We have lost too much fuel to make Salisbury. We are heading for Oman with a cargo and an aircraft worth 22 million dollars and we do not know what's going to happen when we get there."

Sorrel interrupted. "You can forget Oman," she said. "Murphy sold them twenty thousand FN rifles with the wrong calibre ammunition two years ago. No, it's got to be Rhodesia."

Martin ignored her. "Then we'll just have to lose every trace of Interguns from this aircraft. Consignment notes, everything."

"And the logbook, the certificate of registration!" said Harry. He sat watching the control panel, his voice acid with cynicism. "Come on, Martin, every crate in the hold has the company's name stencilled on it."

"Give me an alternative?"

"Dubai, Abu Dhabi, Qatar. We've still got a valid end-user's certificate. We were on our way to Cyprus when we ran into trouble. So we are landing for repairs. Simple."

Martin smiled at him. "You talk crap, my friend. Why the big production at Karachi airport? Like I said, I think we were blown. Every airport in the Middle East will know now that we ignored air traffic control instructions at Karachi. We'll be held pending an inquiry and we'll find ourselves locked away in some Arab jail for months on end."

There was new quality, near to hysteria, in Sorrel's voice as she butted into the conversation again.

"Can't you get it into your heads, you two, that it's Rhodesia that's buying this cargo. They are expecting it. The money's there, waiting for us. You've just somehow got to get to Rhodesia."

The men took no notice.

Martin mused. "What about Israel?"

"No, just look at your chart, my boy," said Harry. "With

our present range we'd need to overfly Iraq, Syria and Jordan carrying a cargo of arms for a suspect destination. No, my love, those guys would not take kindly to our presence in their air space."

They thought for a few moments. Martin could hear Sorrel's deep breathing in his intercom. He half turned to her and said quietly, "Miss Francis, I'm not concerned right at this moment with making money from this flight. My aim is to get the four of us safely on the ground. We don't have enough fuel to get anywhere near Rhodesia. Surely you must realise that."

"Okay, I'll give you the answer," said Harry brightly. "The insurance. The Middle East is full of remote airstrips with no radio, radar or any other facility. Look how easily the Israelis took out Entebbe. Most of these countries are completely deserted except for a few shepherds. So we land, blow this whole pile sky high and leave it to Interguns to sort out."

Martin was considering this when a loud bell started ringing from the control panel.

"Well now," said Martin quietly. "So Mr Murphy has finally woken up. Let's hear what Interguns have to say about this."

*   *   *

As the Corniche reached the second Naples junction on the autostrada, Murphy slowed it and turned off into the grubby outskirts of the city. He stopped on the hard, sandy shoulder of the road.

He continued to talk into the telephone. "I'll be with you in twenty minutes," he said. "Tell Juliet Mike Oscar to circle in its present area and await instructions. Call Bouzet in Paris and tell him to be wide awake when I call him. We have a crisis. Tell Mr Peterson in London that his consignment has been delayed for at least twenty-four hours."

He put the telephone back on to its cradle in the dashboard.

Murphy turned to the girl beside him and woke her gently with his finger-tips on her cheeks.

"Good morning," he said very softly. "The sun is about to rise over Vesuvius. Let's go for a little walk."

*   *   *

The principle Air Attaché to the Soviet Embassy in the Mozambique capital of Lourenço Marques, Major Yefgeni Valentin Uglov sat on the step of his bachelor bungalow in the Embassy compound that morning and watched a small, furry spider amble across the notepad on which he was writing a letter home. It was early morning and already it was far too hot for him. Uglov was fair-haired and his white skin could not take the fierceness of the African sun.

He was not a happy man. His movements were fretful and his face was set in a permanent frown. The Embassy gardens were rich with azaleas and orchids but he disliked them intensely because they attracted insects which he loathed.

He flicked the spider from the writing paper, dabbed a prickly heat rash on his neck with a handkerchief soaked in toilet water, and continued his letter.

Oh my dearest Natasha [he wrote]. Soon it will be winter in our beloved Leningrad and I long for the first chill of winter, for the ice on the Neva, for ballet and the symphony, for The Hermitage and all those things I miss so dearly in my mother country. I dream nightly of walking with you along the Bolshoi Prospect.

Sometimes I despair of Africa. I started here with fifteen trainee pilots, all Mozambiquans and ten MIG 21 fighters. Now I have seven pilots whom I can almost trust and five serviceable aircraft. But what pilots! They are daring in the air, but so dangerous and undisciplined that they terrify me for much of my life.

They ignore all theoretical lessons. They break all the rules of the air. Three days ago, my star pupil, Umboto, flew very low over his village, showing off as usual, and succeeded in setting light to ten thatched roofs with a sudden blast of his after-burners.

I chastised him and he, at least I am sure it was he, took his revenge by filling my cockpit with red ants before an official fly-past in front of the President himself.

Uglov rubbed the seat of his cotton drill trousers and winced with the pain of it. He sipped at a glass of iced tea which was already too warm.

No, my dearest Natasha [he wrote]. It is not easy. Today I am to lecture my pupils on the role of the Proletariat in International Socialism. I despair all the more because I know not one pilot will appear. For when they are not actually flying, it seems the only thing which they enjoy, apart from drinking and wenching, is marching up and down the Via del Revoluzion in their smart new uniforms like children, whistling vulgarly at the girls.

The telephone rang in the bungalow. Major Uglov closed the writing-pad and went indoors.
"Comrade Major Uglov?"
"Yes."
"A message from the Ambassador. You are to report to him immediately."

*   *   *

There was no sign, hardly any indication at all, that this was the Naples office of Interguns Incorporated, a suite of rooms on the top floor of an apartment block overlooking the Piazza Garibaldi, its windows double-glazed against the fierceness of the traffic noise below. Reception was a luxurious office, with armchairs covered in real leather, a small and discreet bar in one corner and a long oaken coffee-table. The walls were soft brown, hung with nineteenth-century Italian ship prints. A miniature antique brass cannon in a glass showcase was the only possible clue to the business transacted in this room.

The office and the city of its location had been well chosen by Murphy. For one thing, Naples was convenient for the host of buyers who came to Interguns from Africa and the Middle East with discreet inquiries for arms. One of the adjoining rooms was filled with samples of small missiles, grenades and various small arms. The reception room itself converted quickly into a preview theatre in which the potential buyer could see any one of three or four hundred types of weapons in actual use on a videotape machine.

The city airport with its lax, easy-going customs and immigration control, was ideal for the comings and goings of buyers, most of whom preferred to travel under questionable documents.

Another room in the office was concerned entirely with communications. It was marked 'Private' and only the most trusted of Interguns employees were allowed to enter it. The three telex machines linked the Naples operation with Interguns offices in Brussels, London and Lausanne. A fourth relayed Reuter's news. A large metal cabinet contained an ultra short wave radio with which Interguns could contact ships and aircraft in any part of the world.

Murphy had driven to Naples that morning to meet with an emissary from Kurdistan who had an interest in a substantial order of anti-tank missiles.

A blonde receptionist sat at a desk topped with leather which matched the armchairs. She handed Murphy a single piece of paper which he studied briefly.

"Get Bouzet," he said to her tersely. He strode across the room and opened the door to the communications room. A dark-haired young man in a short-sleeved shirt was leaning over a telex machine.

"What's the code word for Juliet Mike Oscar?" asked Murphy.

The young man looked at a list on the wall.

"Alabaster."

"Raise Alabaster as soon as you can. Tell them to stand by for instruction. They are not, repeat not, to land at Muscat."

The receptionist was holding the telephone for him when he returned. He grabbed it from her. Murphy was displaying little of the charm which he had shown the previous evening on the Via Veneto.

"Bouzct, listen. I want some action. We have a friend in the Quai d'Orsay. He owes us several favours, right? Okay, this is the favour I need. We've got a Herc with a warm cargo. It left Karachi this morning for the unmentionable place . . ."

Murphy paused and listened. His eyes suddenly flared with anger.

"I know bloody well it's an open line," he said. "There's too much cash at stake to sod about. Tell our friend that I want landing permission for Djibouti. I want repair and re-fuelling facilities and a safe clearance out with no questions. It's the only place they can safely put down. He's got an hour to get this from the Foreign Ministry."

Murphy listened again.

"Now listen, if he argues, tell him that a photostat of all his banking transactions with the Union Bank of Switzerland and ourselves will be on the desk of the French Ambassador in Geneva before cocktail time. Call me straight back." Murphy slammed the telephone down. Only then did he lean over and kiss the receptionist on her cheek.

"Hallo, darling," he said. "Uncle's home."

*   *   *

"Circle, await instructions."

They were doing exactly that at twenty thousand feet over the Arabian sea. They turned steadily to the left, but Martin had allowed the wind at that height to move the aircraft gradually towards the Oman coast.

57

The air was clean now, and Juliet Mike Oscar flew near to stalling speed, easily and lazily. They had cleared the area of low pressure and the storm was behind them. Harry studied a large aviator's chart of Arabia and ringed industriously those possible landing places which they might use. He used a red chinagraph pencil and drew in each of the courses they might possibly need. He hummed softly, working methodically, stopping now and again to take a fuel reading or to skim his eyes along the other instruments.

Stubbles, off the intercom now, tried to explain the intricacies of the engine system to Sorrel. She showed little interest, however. She was nervy and angry and glared across the flight-deck at Martin, who alone appeared relaxed and completely at ease on that flight-deck. He had fallen into the reverie which all flying men know, a time of gentle contemplation from which he could snap back into instant awareness in a matter of micro-seconds. His eyes were closed, his ears muffled against the engine noise.

There had been little enough time for thinking from the moment that they had made the decision for Rhodesia. The girl had produced a set of charts which needed careful study. They could only guess at the weather from a few seemingly casual checks which they were able to take of the Indian Ocean plot in the meteorological office. A crew flying a consignment of weapons, especially of that size, was inevitably given special scrutiny.

Harry had managed to explain away the extra fuel requirement by giving Madrid as the alternative airport on the flight. Had it been day time, the sharp eyes of the Karachi Criminal Investigation Department would almost certainly have pried much harder into her preparations.

It was only now that Martin had time to reflect. He opened his eyes briefly and saw the instrument panel grinning at him. It was then, one hour and twelve minutes into the flight, that the singular and monumental realisation came home to him that he, Martin Gore, son of a distinguished soldier and statesman, was committing treason.

He, Martin Gore. A traitor.

He was suddenly and intensely aware of the navy blue British passport number 823727 which lay in the flight bag beside him. The Smith Government of Rhodesia was illegal. Smith had rebelled against the British Government. Christ, he thought. The charges they will throw.

Aiding and abetting and giving comfort to Her Majesty's enemies. That would be the first of them. It was a Tower of London job, that was for sure. Martin Gore, you have succeeded in bringing disgrace on one of the greatest families of this realm. No punishment can be too great for you ... I have, however, taken into account the hurt and humiliation which you have rendered upon a fine family ... That would be the crime, of course, letting the side down. The Establishment got very cross when one of their own went out of line ... The sentence of this court is that you shall go to prison for thirty years.

The Hercules jolted slightly in a small patch of turbulence. Martin opened his eyes again and saw Harry making a minuscule trim adjustment.

Thirty years. Bloody hell, he thought. He closed his eyes again and shuddered slightly. And then an even more overwhelming thought arrived in his mind. The penalty for treason in Britain was death. Martin felt very cold for a second or so.

Bloody hell, indeed. Oh Gore, Gore, you tiresome impetuous twit, he considered. You've jumped right into this one, my son. Just like all the other times. Pilots are supposed to be cautious men who approach each situation with a logical analysis. And you, you great hairy chump, what do you do? For the sake of a few lousy dollars you are prepared to throw the whole damn lot away.

"Six hours' flying time left at this speed and height."

"Thanks, Harry."

If, he thought. Here goes If Sequence number 530. If I hadn't made the biggest homemade firework in the history of the college, I would have gone to Oxford and joined the Foreign Office and I wouldn't have needed to have joined the Air Force. If I hadn't joined the Air Force I wouldn't have been able to punch the Group Captain. Mind you, the bastard deserved it. And if I hadn't taken that job with Idi Amin, I wouldn't have hit the Sergeant and ended up in that Kampala nick with my balls tied to the chair with piano wire.

Harry touched his sleeve. The co-pilot was pointing to the radarscope in front of them. On the extreme top he could see a yellowish line beginning to appear.

"The Yemen coast," said Harry.

Martin looked at his watch. "We'll give Murphy ten minutes," he said. "If he hasn't come up with something by then we'll operate the doomsday business and blow the whole bloody lot up somewhere in the desert."

Harry shrugged his shoulders. Martin went back to Sequence If.

And if, he realised savagely, if I had not put every penny I had on a twelve to one shot in the Derby, I wouldn't have needed this bloody job. Your whole life, Mr Gore, has been governed, directed and generally buggered up by your own impulsive nature.

So what could they do about it?

*   *   *

One hundred and forty miles above the Arabian Sea, a Samov satellite rolled on to its belly from which it had been using a small, wide-angle lens to transmit weather information. Now, two alloy hatches slid open to reveal a new lens, 800 millimetres of it, which began to protrude itself obscenely towards the earth's surface.

A computer in Odessa which had ordered the change of lens now gave a further series of instructions to the miniature computer in the satellite. The lens began to follow the estimated track of Juliet Mike Oscar. At each tenth of a degree the camera shutter behind it opened and the image was transmitted immediately to appear on a television screen in Odessa. Several technicians and two satellite intelligence observers watched each changing frame on a series of repeater screens.

When the satellite had passed well beyond the speed and range capacities of the C 130, a fresh set of instructions was passed through the computers.

The lens re-traced its track, this time one degree to the west, and again, as it failed to find anything except a few freighters and the occasional fishing dhow, it widened the area of its search along either side of the estimated track.

It took just under ten minutes to find Juliet Mike Oscar. It appeared first as a smudgy dot. The lens was adjusted until the shape of the aircraft came into fine focus.

*   *   *

Natalia Rogov was eating a lightly boiled egg in the Foreign Ministry canteen when she saw the air force officer crossing towards her through a mass of empty breakfast tables. He was one of the officers who had been sitting at the committee table, a young colonel with a pleasing, open face. He bowed slightly before he sat at her table.

He was faintly embarrassed by the scent and sexuality of this woman, being himself married to a rather plain and square-shaped woman from Kiev, and he found difficulty in looking directly into her eyes.

"We have traced the suspect aircraft, Comrade," he said. "Its behaviour is somewhat erratic, not as your estimate predicted."

Natalia tore a piece of bread from a brown roll and smeared it with butter.

"Some coffee, Colonel?"

"No, thank you."

"They eat well in this Ministry," she said. "Our canteen at the Lenin Institute is like a railway station snack bar. In what way erratic?"

"It is heading in a curious direction."

"Towards Rhodesia?"

The Colonel opened his brief-case and took out a set of photographs from a folder. He handed them to Natalia. They were still moist from the high-speed development process.

"Not apparently. It is a good fifteen degrees off the course it would need. And it would seem most likely that it has not enough fuel to get to Salisbury."

"So where then?"

"Look carefully at the outer port engine. Satellite Analysis are reasonably certain that there are traces of a fire."

Natalia looked closely at the silhouette of the aircraft.

"What, then, is its destination?"

"That is anyone's guess."

Natalia lit a cigarette and tapped her Fabergé lighter on the bare plastic table. She was nervous.

"My head, it seems, is on the block." She smiled. "The entire Praesidium is watching this."

She tapped Juliet's profile with a long, carefully manicured finger-nail. "It's all on my recommendation."

"You could not know anything about an emergency in flight."

"Tchakev does not like me," she said quietly. "He keeps the dossiers and he has Comrade Gromyko's ear."

"You still have the air force," said the Colonel.

*   *   *

Now she breasted the sky with matronly confidence, flying through air which was thin and cold and free from turbulence. Her crew had relaxed. Stubbles had climbed into the spare bunk at the rear of the flight-deck and was half dozing while his ears continued to monitor the sound of Juliet's three remaining engines.

Martin had ordered the engineer to rest. He had been up

for most of the previous night repairing the broken oil feed and attending to countless other small jobs, and he would be needed again almost immediately after landing to attend to the replacement of number one engine.

Harry, in the co-pilot's seat, was maintaining a careful watch on the air waves, listening for any further mention of themselves. Earlier he had heard the Karachi controller order an alert and request a search for unscheduled zero zero two. He had appeased the controller with a short and thrifty message in which he had said, "Unscheduled proceeding."

The controller's acknowledgement was laconic with only a hint of his true feelings.

"Thank you, unscheduled, and good day."

The emphasis was on the 'good'.

Harry grinned. He was flying an aircraft which had disobeyed a clear instruction, which had broken rigid radar direction, noise abatement laws and which had caused an air-sea rescue alert. Christ, the paperwork, he thought. Copies to Civil Aviation Board, Pakistani Civil Aviation Authority, Air Registration Board, the International Airline Pilots' Association and God knows who else.

Martin and Sorrel sat on the cabin floor under Stubbles' bunk. He had taken her off the intercom system and was talking loudly into her ear over the engine noise. The others did not notice but he was gripping her arm firmly. She was looking pale and there was defiance in her eyes. His face was taught, the thin scar accentuated.

"Now what in hell's name is Murphy playing at?" he growled. "Why the switch, why that business at Karachi? Christ knows, this is a hairy enough adventure without that sort of thing."

"What do you mean?"

"A controller tries to abort us in the middle of a take-off roll — that's unheard of, did you know that? Then fighters. We were blown from the very beginning. Now, who blew?"

She was angry but she was becoming more and more frightened by the fury in his eyes.

"How would I know?" she said quietly. "Would you let go of my arm. You're hurting."

"I'll spank your pretty little arse if you don't explain one or two things."

"Like what?"

"Like, does Ragnelli know about this flight?"

"How would I know?"

"You *would* know. You do the paper work. Murphy can't so much as belch without you knowing about it."

Martin was gripping the girl's arm fiercely now. "Now listen," he was saying. "I'm an English gentleman, believe it or not. But I'll tell you this, young lady, I'm quite willing to shake you like a terrier shakes a rat until I get the truth."

Sorrel pulled away from him, snatching her arm free. It was her turn to be livid now.

"Just try it, baby," she shouted.

Martin saw Harry turn from the controls. There was an uncomprehending look on the co-pilot's face.

Sorrel pulled herself to her feet.

"Oh no, buster," she yelled. Her voice was harsh and falsetto. "Tougher men than you have tried to beat me about. Just remember one thing and keep it uppermost in that shitty chauvinistic mind of yours. I know just how broke you are and how much you need that money. Come to think of it Interguns has a dossier on you Martin Gore that your creditors would just love to have in their pudgy little hands. And just one other thing. Like I said, it's cash they're paying at the other end in crisp green US Treasury bills. And the only way that you're going to get that cash is by my releasing an agreed coded signal to the banks that are holding the buyer's money. So don't push me."

Martin reached up and grabbed her arm again and pulled her heavily down on the floor. He gripped her even harder now. She squealed.

"I asked you a question," he barked at her. "Does Ragnelli know about this load?"

The strength of his grip made her wince. Tears of pain

appeared in her eyes. Then she began to cry freely and fluently.

"No, he doesn't," she wailed. "Murphy is free-lancing."

Martin ignored the tears. He became very thoughtful for a few seconds.

"You mean the Mafia doesn't know. Their weapons and their plane? Oh, Jesus Christ what have we let ourselves in for now?"

He rose to his feet. The girl stayed on the floor of the flight-deck and sobbed into the crook of her folded arms.

Martin returned to the captain's seat.

"Did you get the gist of all that?" he said to a bewildered looking co-pilot. "Not merely is this the hottest cargo we could be carrying under International Law but Murphy has heisted it from the mob. Harry, dear boy, this whole bloody flight is doomed. Why did we ever get tied up with that bastard Ragnelli in the first place?"

Harry shrugged his shoulders. Then he looked over Martin's shoulders.

"It ain't just the mob who is after us," he said grimly. "We've got company, Martin."

He gestured with his finger out of the side panel.

Flying on a parallel course, two hundred feet from their wing tip, was a long, graceful military jet with the bright red star of the Red Air Force on its pencil-shaped fuselage. Martin could see its captain peering out at them. The jet dipped and flew underneath them. He felt Juliet buck in the wash of its turbulence. He clipped off the auto pilot and flew her manually and watched, as a moment or so later the other aircraft resumed its level flight, this time on their port side.

"What is it?"

Harry fingered quickly through a recognition manual.

"It's a Myasishev Four," he said. "NATO code name Bison B. Long-range maritime reconnaissance. Pretty, isn't she?"

"What does the bastard want?"

"There's a whole swarm of Russians not so very far from here in Socotra, quite a big base they have."

Martin looked more closely at the Myasishev. There were several domes under its fuselage and he knew that they were filled with complex electronic equipment.

He saw the Russian co-pilot pointing at the microphone which he held in his left hand.

"Listen in," he said. Harry turned to the air-to-air frequency.

A deep, heavily accented voice was talking to them. "Good afternoon, Juliet Mike Oscar. Do you require assistance?" it was saying.

"What do I tell him?"

"Tell him no."

"No thank you, Comrade, all's well," said Harry in a friendly voice and pushed the 'receive' button.

"Juliet Mike Oscar, what is your destination?"

Harry was about to answer when he felt Martin's hand gripping his arm.

"Tell him Addis Ababa."

Harry relayed the message and signed off. The other aircraft slid away to port, losing height gradually.

Martin watched it and said quietly into the intercom.

"Did you paint out all the markings last night?"

"Every one. Wings, top and bottom, fuselage and fin."

Martin was silent for a few moments.

"So how did that bastard know our call sign?" he asked.

"Shit, we *are* hot."

* * *

The wind which had blown oven-hot across the desert all morning had dropped now, and the ancient city of Djibouti lay bleached and petrified under the fiery white noontide sun. The Tricolors drooped listlessly from public buildings already emptied of most of their bureaucrats. Few would move in that city from now until the cool of the evening. Traffic had ceased to bark along the dust-caked streets and the ebony-coloured gendarme in the traffic control box on the Avenue des Héros was wiping the sweat from the rim of his *kepi* before going off duty. A tape-recorded *muezzin* wailed the faithful to prayer from a glacial minaret on the Mosque of Omar, and the only other sounds were the crashing of shop shutters as the Levantine traders locked away their camel saddles, hand-carved ivory and tawdry souvenirs, and the slamming of cashboxes as the Armenians in the dark and mysterious money-souk locked away fortunes in grubby dollars, francs and pounds and all the garish currencies of the East.

Soon Djibouti would die for four torpid, sweltering hours as it had done each afternoon since pre-history. It is a city built in the very pit of the cauldron of Arabia, in which the greatest luxury is a cooling wind from the sea which in summer is a rarity indeed, in which there is no respite from the glowing heat except a siesta, or death itself.

But three men did not sleep this day.

In his whitewashed villa on the mud-brown hills overlooking Djibouti, Alexander Turok, the Soviet Vice Consul to the French territory of Afars et Issis, of which Djibouti is the capital, studied a message which he had recently received in the daily noon transmission from Moscow. It was a short message, but it took him some time to decode it for his eyes kept filling with sweat and his steel-rimmed spectacles steamed up continually as he leaned over his deciphering manual.

Turok was an elderly man with a large, steel-grey, Stalin-like moustache of which he was inordinately proud; he did all things methodically including the copious drinking of vodka which had led to this particular diplomatic posting.

He finished decoding and went into his bathroom where he took a towel and soaked it in cold water before wiping his head and neck free of perspiration. Then he went to his kitchen and took a bottle of Moscovitch vodka from the freezing compartment. He poured himself a generous measure and swallowed it in one noisy gulp. Only then did he return to his office to read the message.

It read:

ATTENTION TUROK. URGENT. SOVINTELLIGENCE INDICATES C 130 AIRCRAFT FORMERLY OF US AIR FORCE EN ROUTE FOR RHODESIA LIKELY TO LAND AT DJIBOUTI APPROXIMATELY 12.30 HOURS LOCAL TIME TODAY TO EFFECT REPAIRS. THIS AIRCRAFT IS CARRYING A SUSPECT CARGO PROBABLY ARMS. YOU ARE INSTRUCTED TO:

1. VERIFY THE FINAL DESTINATION OF THIS AIRCRAFT AND REPORT IMMEDIATELY;

2. STATE NATURE OF DAMAGE;

3. REPORT ON ALL CO-OPERATION RECEIVED FROM AUTHORITIES;

4. HAVING ESTABLISHED THESE FACTS BEGIN IMMEDIATE PREPARATIONS FOR SPONTANEOUS DEMONSTRATIONS BY POPULAR FRONT ORGANISATIONS IN YOUR TERRITORY TO COMMENCE ON NOTIFICATION=LITVINOFF.

Turok read the message again. His hands were shaking violently. He returned to the refrigerator and poured another, equally large, vodka. Then he picked up his telephone and ordered his secretary and the rest of his small staff to remain on duty. Few priority cables arrived at Djibouti. Cables from Litvinoff, the head of the KGB, were rare indeed.

Turok went out to the patio of the villa and the fierce heat hit him as he looked out over the sleeping city. He saw beyond the docks the shape of an aircraft appear from the heat haze and he heard the soft throb of its three engines.

*   *   *

Charles Victor de Marchant, the plenipotentiary Minister of the Interior for Afars et Issis, also heard the engines and went to the balcony of his Ministry, a handsome and

Napoleonic-styled building in the centre of Djibouti.

Juliet Mike Oscar's undercarriage dropped into landing position as he watched.

De Marchant swore softly at the aircraft as it wheeled south towards Loyada airport.

The Minister, a small, fussy man with a belly which bulged over the waistline of his pinstriped trousers, picked up one of the several telephones at his desk and called the Foreign Legion garrison on the outskirts of the city.

He read, once again, a cable which he had just received from the Foreign Ministry in Paris.

⁂

The airport slept, too. Only on very rare occasions did any pilot elect to land at midday in Djibouti, when the heat rose in great glistening columns from the concrete runway, distorting all distances and making the air thin and weak and treacherous.

The airport manager's office was locked. The ticket desks were deserted. Fire crews slept in the little shade that they could find. Even the beggars and freelance porters had disappeared in that curious way in which only Arabs can suddenly melt into nothing at any given time of the day or night.

The duty controller had left the tower in charge of his trainee assistant, a young Arab who sat alone now in the control tower trying hard to master the English grammar essential to his elected profession.

The heat, in spite of the air-conditioning, became too much, even for him, and he was quietly dozing when Harry Black's voice cut through the loudspeaker system.

"Djibouti tower this is unscheduled transport Juliet Mike Oscar. We are ten miles from you at zero one six requesting clearance to land. Over."

The young Arab shook himself and yawned. Assuming a

nonchalance which he admired so much in his French tutor, he switched on the microphone on the desk in front of him and said in a bored voice, "Yeah, okay."

*   *   *

"What the hell does that mean?" said Martin, frowning.
"I read it that we are clear to land."
The coastline and the hills behind loomed close now. The city gleamed in a brilliant white dot in the yellowish brown coastal plain. They were losing height steadily as Harry carefully adjusted the propeller levers.
"We could wake him with a Mayday call," he said. "After all, we've only three engines."
"Low profile," said Martin. "The less noise we make and the less trouble we cause the better. We've got clearance. That's all that matters. Okay, let's start approach checks."
Martin glanced behind. Stubbles was in the engineer's seat reading a Dick Tracy comic. Sorrel was sleeping lightly in the bunk. Stubbles had taken pity and poured her a large whisky. Martin chose to let her sleep.
"TD valve switches."
"Auto and locked."
Thirty minutes earlier, Martin and Harry had been playing poker for quarters and dimes using a biscuit tin balanced on the auto pilot for the stake money. Now they were airmen again, terse and concentrating. Stubbles had stowed the comic and was holding his engineer's checklist. His growth of beard was irritating him and he scratched his chin continually.
"Radome anti-icing."
"Off."
They ran quickly through the rest of the checks. The altimeters were set and Harry studied the approach map to Djibouti from his aviator's manual.

70

"Djibouti tower. Juliet Mike Oscar. We are four miles from you at zero one six degrees. Can you give landing conditions, please."

There was a very long pause.

"Yeah, okay."

The two pilots waited. Now they were almost over the city and could distinguish individual buildings. They could see the short, narrow runway to the south.

"Djibouti tower. We are waiting for wind and ground temperatures."

Another long pause. "Oh yeah. There is no wind. Ground temperature . . . hold on."

Harry could see Martin mouthing obscenities as he waited impatiently.

"Forty-four degrees, nine nine four millibars."

Martin spoke. "Djibouti tower, thank you. I take it we land west to east?"

"Yeah, okay."

"Jesus." Martin shook his head in disbelief. "Pre-landing check. Flaps."

"As required."

"Gear down."

"Gear down. Three greens. Checked and nose wheel centred."

By the time they had completed the checks the aircraft had passed over the city. Martin took her well inland and at six thousand feet she leaped violently as she met the up-draughts over the hills.

It was not an easy landing. As they turned towards the outer marker and began their final descent, Juliet bucked and fought and suddenly dropped violently as they crossed the hills again into an area of low pressure.

Their descent was fast and Harry changed pitch continually and held the air brakes until the last possible moment. Martin's eyes appeared almost closed as he strained to see the runway through the heat shimmer.

His hands made deft, microscopic movements on the control column. His right leg ached as he maintained a constant battle using the rudder to counter the uneven engine pull.

They had no alternative but to hit the runway hard. They had been close indeed to over-shooting and Harry rammed the two inboard propellers into reverse as soon as the massive plane bounced for the second time. He needed no command.

They had used half the runway before Martin was able to apply the brakes. It was a desperate and dangerous moment. The two inboard engines, even at the maximum power and pitch, had little slowing effect in that heat. They saw the sea racing towards them at the end of the runway. Too much brake at that moment on that fiercely hot runway would have shredded all six tyres in a matter of seconds.

Harry was yelling the ground speed. He did not hide his fear.

With five hundred feet of runway left, Martin braked. Juliet Mike Oscar came to a shuddering, lurching, teetering standstill with twenty yards of concrete left.

Book Two

COLONEL-GENERAL YURI IVAN LITVINOFF was a huge, bluff, merry-looking man whose only vice was the chainsmoking of Havana cigars which he indulged throughout his long working day. He was a family man who was devoted to his wife and four children and a terrier dog. He enjoyed playing practical jokes and his greatest pride was a complete collection of Laurel and Hardy movies which he ran over and over again in his weekend *dacha* on the Moskva river.

During the week he ran the biggest intelligence and counter-intelligence organisation in the world. Litvinoff was the Director of the KGB and, as such, the third most powerful man after the Secretary of the Communist Party and the President, in Soviet Russia. He was in fact invulnerable, omnipotent and entirely secure within that system, and he could thus afford to play practical jokes and to maintain a benign, Pickwickian exterior to the rest of the world. He was doing that soon after noon that day to an angry, lividly angry, Natalia Rogov who was pacing up and down the length of his office, gesticulating with her long tapering hands and fingers, her voice shrill and strident. Her lithe body trembled with fury as she faced him.

It was an extraordinary scene. In Moscow it was incredible. Secretaries in the anteroom stopped talking and typing and listened with growing incredulity. Here was a young woman, known to be suspect for her western bourgeois tastes and allegedly decadent habits, openly abusing a man who, with one push of a button on his desk, could have her imprisoned, certified to a lunatic asylum, or dispatched for years

75

of forced labour in the Virgin lands. No one raised his voice to the head of the KGB. Certainly no one ever screamed at him in this fashion.

"Is it not possible for your heavy-handed, big-footed, clumsy operatives to stay out of anything?" she was shouting. "Can't you see that you are destroying a carefully thought out plan for totally discrediting the United States' foreign policy in Africa? It was my idea and I was backed by my minister and by Comrade Brezhnev himself. It was working well — and now *you* have to muscle in. You alert every agent in Africa, especially that drunken oaf Turok. The aircraft will turn back and the whole operation will have been a total waste of time and effort."

Litvinoff looked at the girl through huge blue eyes and removed the cigar from the centre of his mouth. He chuckled. His jowls shook.

"You have your father's temper, little Natalia," he said. "It is fortunate that you have your mother's good looks."

"Don't patronise me!" she shouted. "I am thirty-five years old. I am not a child any more."

A mock sternness came into his voice.

"If I hadn't known you as a child, little Natalia, and if I had not fought with your father in Leningrad and eaten rats cooked by your mother during the siege, then you would have been well chastised by now."

She flushed and sat down in a chair opposite him. She forced a smile.

"What do you mean?"

"Child," he said, tapping an inch of ash from the end of the cigar. "You have succeeded in breaking every rule in the KGB book. You have acted independently and you know there is no room for private enterprise in the intelligence area. We leave that sort of entrepreneuring to the Americans. You have even set up your own lines of communication, tried to appoint your own agents. Surely you must realise that every move you have made has been monitored by the KGB, that I have had daily, almost hourly reports on your activities."

"Then why did you let me continue? And why did the minister give his support?"

"Because, dearest Natalia, you were doing well. Some of my officers complained bitterly about your involvement. You are hardly the most popular person in Moscow at this moment. I decided to let you have your head."

"Why?"

"Because it was a brilliant idea. And you are quite right about the heavy-handedness of some of my staff. There is a secondary reason, Comrade niece. It would suit my purposes very well to have you in this department in a senior grade. If you had succeeded in this operation, I could have transferred you without any charge of nepotism. In my position I need people around me whom I can trust absolutely."

Litvinoff stood at his desk and his vast bulk towered over the girl. There were five rows of medal ribbons on his simple, grey uniform. Natalia stared at them, trying hard to assimilate what her uncle had been saying.

"I am doing an important job at the Institute."

The big man guffawed as he walked around the big picture window and surveyed the city.

"Writing learned papers, greeting delegations of tribesmen in their multicoloured nightgowns? An important job? Nonsense, child. Here you can act. With your intellect and intelligence and with your specialised knowledge of Africa you can have more influence on that continent in one week than the imperialists Cecil Rhodes or Smuts ever dreamed of in their lifetime."

"But the KGB?"

"Do not disparage the KGB. It is a front line army, niece. While you sit with your books and slide-rules and plan grand strategies, we are in the field preparing the ground. You are young and active and you would be best employed in such an organisation."

"Then why interfere with my operation now?"

He turned to her. He walked over and stood behind her and put his arms on her shoulders.

"Because things have gone wrong. The aeroplane is not in flight over Mozambique. It has made a forced landing in Djibouti. We will make the maximum propaganda use of this. And Africa will soon know of the US duplicity within a matter of hours."

Natalia was immediately angry again. She shook his hands away.

"Comrade Colonel-General, that is exactly the wrong approach. The Americans can lie their way out of that easily. The missiles could be going anywhere. We have absolutely no proof that they are going to Rhodesia."

"The KGB does not insist on proof."

"You talk of a day or so of trouble, Comrade uncle. A few American embassies get stoned, maybe burned down. So, that's commonplace."

"And we embarrass the French. Djibouti is very sensitive. We have worked hard there."

She stood and tried to gain the maximum height against his.

"Djibouti is a pimple. We can squeeze that at any time. If we can prove to the world that the Americans are smuggling arms into Rhodesia, if we can produce those missiles, we can prove them to be liars in the face of international opinion. The effect on Africans in Rhodesia itself and South Africa would be unbelievable."

Litvinoff walked back to his desk and relit his cigar. He gazed at Natalia reflectively as he puffed it back into life.

"Can you be sure that it will be forced down? There is every chance, surely, that with that load of arms it will simply blow into a billion fragments and then there will be no evidence."

"I am assured by the Red Air Force that it can be done."

Litvinoff became pensive again.

"You make a lot of sense, Comrade niece. Very well, I will try to keep my hunting dogs in their kennels for a few more hours. But remember that they are hungry for your blood. And remember too, my dearest Natalia, that if we succeed it is the KGB which takes the credit."

*   *   *

No one moved on that flight-deck. No one spoke for fifteen full seconds. The three crew members sat frozen and gazed with empty, vacant faces at the rocky beach immediately in front of the aircraft and the vividly blue sea which beckoned beyond. Harry kept his hand on the engine condition levers because he knew that it would begin to shake uncontrollably if he moved it.

Martin tasted blood on the side of his tongue. He had bitten his lip in the intense concentration of that approach and landing. Stubbles sat open-mouthed. Sorrel had woken on the initial thump and she was only vaguely aware of the real danger which had faced them. But she sensed the tension and wanted to say something trite and silly which would make these three statues move.

Stubbles said it instead.

"Well, yes," he said, mocking the voice of a flying instructor. "That's one way of doing it, Captain."

The engines settled to the soft whine of ground idle.

Martin's face broke very slowly into a wide grin. He looked at Harry. "Brother, if you could see your face. It isn't just pale, it's transparent."

Harry risked taking his hand off the lever. It did not shake. He felt his whole body shuddering, however, with relief. He smiled.

"You dangerous bastard," he said. "No bloody wonder that you can't get a job with a civilised airline."

They began to laugh. Nervous, childish laughter which spilled the fear and agonising taughtness from them. Stubbles thumped his hands on his knees. Martin whooped like a cowboy. Harry kept saying, "Christ Almighty".

They were close to hysteria when a new voice joined them.

The accent was heavy, French. It was an acid and demanding voice.

"This is Djibouti ground control. Unidentified aircraft you are instructed to leave the runway and turn right on to the apron and park after two hundred yards. You are to switch off your engines and wait in that position. You are not to leave the aircraft under any circumstances."

They stopped laughing. There was menace in this voice. They did not like it.

"Friendly," said Harry.

"After landing checks," said Martin grimly. "Flaps?"

"Up."

"Navigation equipment?"

"Off."

Martin glanced out of his side panel before taxiing off the runway. There were two jeeps parked at each wing tip. Machine guns were clipped on to the bodywork. They were trained onto the flight-deck of the aircraft by two unsmiling and entirely businesslike foreign légionnaires.

*   *   *

Murphy walked briskly along the Corso Umberto and turned into the maze of dingy streets which lead to the Capitano Palace and the hotel suite where the girl was waiting for him. It was a hot, humid day and Naples was vibrantly alive. Each doorway had a different sound, of backroom industry, of shrill gossip, of family squabble, of the soft *senta* of pimps and whores; and each a different smell, of leather, of bread, of laundry steam, of garlic and cheap perfume. It was a walk to take slowly and savour. But Murphy moved quickly, side-stepping the street vendors and tarts. He was in a hurry.

He had driven into Naples that morning with every intention of losing himself until Juliet Mike Oscar had delivered her load in Salisbury and the money had been released from the National Bank of Switzerland where it was being lodged in his personal account in the Liechtenstein Hangl Bank.

He would make four million dollars from this deal.

He could afford to pay a hundred and fifty thousand to the crew.

Had Martin Gore not insisted on the girl being on the flight, Murphy would have ensured that the crew would have seen little of this money. For one thing he disliked Martin Gore. He disliked most Englishmen but Gore was a special case. He was smooth and hard and a professional. He was also too honest for Murphy's liking.

And Gore had asked far too many questions about Ragnelli and the organisation.

The deal had been arranged in a matter of hours. The two envoys from the Smith Government were desperate for these weapons. Smith and his government were being gradually forced to bow to world opinion. A British minister was, even at this moment, flying between various black capitals in Southern Africa. A settlement was becoming a distinct possibility.

With these arms safely in his possession, Smith would be in a far stronger bargaining position.

The Rhodesians had relied until now on South Africa for arms. It seemed quite certain that the American Government would persuade a worried South African Government to stop military aid.

No wonder the two Rhodesians had been keen to part with such large sums of money.

He had planned this day with thoroughness. By noon he had hoped to have brought off the deal with the Kurds for ten million dollars worth of anti-tank missiles. That, in fact, had turned out to be disastrous. The Kurds could not prove the availability of the necessary money and he had almost literally thrown them out of the office.

He had planned then to go to the suite in the hotel where the girl whom he had met at Rome Airport the previous evening was waiting for him.

He had allowed two hours for making love to her and when that had been completed he would begin to disappear from the face of the earth for six months.

He had leased his villa at a satisfactory rent which would be paid into a numbered account in Luxembourg. He had sold the Camargue for a pleasing profit to an oil broker in Cannes and the Corniche, his favourite toy, was already being offered in a Naples showroom at a sensible loss for a quick sale.

By mid-afternoon he had planned to be on one of the several ferries which ply passengers between Naples and the Island of Ischia. Until then he was in considerable danger. He knew that. If they found him, Ragnelli's operation would eat him up and spit him out.

But even here, in this city which was saturated with *Mafiosa,* he reckoned he was safe for a few hours at least before the word was out.

He and the girl would walk to the harbour, and in Ischia where there were no customs and few questions they would be aboard a seventy foot chartered motor yacht within a matter of minutes and away into the open Mediterranean. The yacht was well provisioned, and he had made arrangements to moor in the Turkish sector of Cyprus where few Europeans were allowed. Money, again, had changed hands.

At nine-thirty, when the banks opened on the following morning, James Murphy would be a dollar millionaire with a new identity and a forged Irish passport to prove it.

He had made too many enemies in the past two or three years. It was an undeniable hazard of that lucrative trade. At least two Arab kingdoms had placed him on their list for elimination, largely because they were close to war with each other and Murphy had been supplying them with substantial quantities of weapons with which to fight each other. The British Special Branch had accumulated a file on him several inches thick and they were ready to move for his extradition.

It was time to be moving on, he had reckoned. And Ragnelli would have to take his place in the queue for his execution.

The news from Juliet Mike Oscar had shattered him momentarily. But he had recovered well.

The French Foreign Office had been dubious about allowing the aircraft to land on French territory, but his contact was a persuasive man.

It had taken him less than an hour to locate a replacement engine. It was one of twelve which had been newly reconditioned for the Greek Air Force by a private engineering firm in Piraeus and, by mid-morning it had been crated and was on its way to the International Airport.

This part had been simple. He was paying several thousand dollars over the odds, certainly, but he had saved himself several days of argument with Greek bureaucracy. This engine would, in turn, be replaced by the damaged engine from Djibouti. The serial numbers would be changed and the Greeks and the Air Registration Board would be none the wiser.

The Athenian handling agent had managed to get the engine on to an early Misrair freighting flight to Cairo while another agent, under the promise of a substantial bonus, would personally supervise its loading on to the ageing Super Constellation which plied the Red Sea local service.

A delay of twenty-four hours. That was not bad. The Rhodesian buyer in London, Peterson, had whined, and Murphy himself could not be one hundred per cent sure of the money until the aircraft touched down. But nonetheless he walked with a confident bounce from the heat of the piazza into the cool hotel lobby. The concierge bowed slightly as he told Murphy that the *Signora* had taken the key to the suite an hour before.

Murphy was already feeling a strong tingle of desire as he pressed the button in the antique caged elevator. There is nothing quite like a feeling of danger to get a man really eager for it, he was thinking, and his pace quickened even more along the heavy pile carpet which led to the suite.

A 'Do Not Disturb' sign hung on the big brass door knob.

Murphy smiled. She was ready, just as he had requested.

He opened the door and went into the sitting room. The bedroom door was two inches open.

It was only then that he saw the man sitting in a deep armchair in a corner behind him. The man was heavily tanned, with a skinny body like those of the workmen in the street outside. He wore faded blue jeans and a white string vest. There were splashes of blood on the vest.

The man trained a small Beretta pistol on Murphy's groin.

"Good morning, Murphy," said the man. He flicked the gun possibly a centimetre away from Murphy's genitals towards the bedroom. "Take a look at her. You're next. That is unless you can get Mr Ragnelli his aeroplane back."

*   *   *

"You will switch off engines and you will leave the aircraft while it is inspected."

They liked his voice even less.

Martin glanced through the windshield. There were three jeeps in view now, one of them parked directly beneath him. He could see the rifling on the barrel of the Schmeitzer machine gun. The black légionnaire behind it peered directly along the sights at his head.

"Cut everything except the cooling system and open the doors," he said. His voice was weary and resigned.

Martin rose slowly and reluctantly and clambered down from the flight-deck, on to the steps and into heat which made him feel sick and strangely cold as his body thermostat fought to adjust. Harry followed and then Stubbles, who blinked owl-like into the fierceness of that sun.

"Hey, it's the real thing," he said. "D'ya ever see *Beau geste*? That's how they dressed in *Beau Geste*."

"Shut up."

"Yeah, that was a great movie. Gary Cooper. They all wore those crazy hats."

"Cool it."

Martin was looking round. A fourth jeep was parked under the tailplane. A fifth was racing along the apron leaving a spectacular trail of dust. This jeep circled the parked aircraft twice clearly for dramatic effect, the driver making his tyres squeal continually, and then stopped a few yards from the waiting airmen. A blond man in a khaki shirt and shorts, wearing a *kepi* with a brilliantly white sun-shade over his neck and sporting the three bars of a captain, climbed out with relaxed ease and walked across towards them. A cigarette was hanging from his mouth.

There was an arrogant assurance about his walk. Martin found himself clenching his right hand into an instinctive fist. He looked at the massive holster on the man's thigh and unclenched his fingers. Here, he thought, is a one hundred per cent French pig who is going to ride me and Martin Gore is going to have to take it, aren't you Martin Gore?

The captain stood in front of him and looked at all three of them in turn. There was dislike in his eyes. He faced Harry.

"Who are you?"

"I am the captain of this aircraft," snapped Martin. "And I am telling you that there is an international law that no one smokes within fifty yards of a parked aeroplane. That means anyone. So take that dog-end out of your mouth and kill it."

"*You* are ordering *me*?"

"Spit it out or I'll take it out."

They were glaring at each other.

Great start to a new acquaintance, Martin was thinking. Ten minutes from now and you'll be begging this bastard for a spanner and a gantry and help to change the engine. So what do you do? You square up to the pig.

The Frenchman took the cigarette out of his mouth. He blew the acrid caporal smoke in a thin stream towards

Martin's face. And he replaced it in his mouth.

"I must inform you that you are all three of you to be held and the aircraft impounded while inquiries are being made. What is the nature of your cargo?"

"The cigarette, monsieur."

"If you must choose to be obstructive, Captain" ... The Frenchman managed to combine disbelief and contempt into the word 'captain' ... "I shall hold you at gunpoint and you may find yourselves sitting in the sun for the next few hours. Your flight documents, please."

"The cigarette," Martin was shouting now. "That lousy cigarette." Harry touched his arm and he pushed him away angrily.

The Frenchman unclipped the holster. He had become bored with this Englishman. And then Sorrel stepped out of the hatch.

She had made-up her face and she had changed into a simply cut dress of white cotton with a neck-line which plunged to her waist. She smiled at everybody.

The effect of that frail, feminine body in that acutely masculine set-up was monumental. She looked at the men with an almost childlike innocence. She had special eyes for the Frenchman. The innocent eyes of a fawn who had found the hunter.

"Hallo," she said. "Having trouble?"

The cigarette disappeared from the Frenchman's mouth immediately. He straightened his back and saluted automatically.

"Mam'selle," he said. His eyes ranged several times up and down her body, pausing at the whiteness of her breasts and then settling on her eyes, which remained wide open and questioning.

Martin breathed again. "Harry, get the papers," he said quietly. He was trying to read Sorrel's mind but could only guess her scenario. "Captain, this is Miss Francis who is a passenger."

The Frenchman did not hear him. His eyes had not left the girl for one instant.

Martin looked down and saw, with satisfaction, that the Frenchman had ground his cigarette, half smoked, on to the surface of the runway.

*   *   *

Murphy pushed the door open very slowly. He smelled the carnage at once, a curious, subtle scent of blood and flesh which was almost overpowered by the other scent of perfume and toilet water that the girl had been using. She was dead. She lay spreadeagled on the bed, naked, her body vivid with violet-coloured bruises. Her neck had been sliced cleanly under her right ear and the blood must have fountained from the artery because it covered much of the bed and the wall behind it. There was no repose in her death. Her face was a loathsome, grotesque mask of terror.

Murphy had seen a lot of horror. He had created it, encouraged it and had achieved a considerable reputation for it. In his time he had ordered the massacre of whole villages in the Congo and he had used a few tribeswomen for target practice. He had ordered his men to burn down a large school and to machine gun down the children as they ran from the flames. He had shot his own men, sometimes in the head to kill them instantly, sometimes, as a punishment, in the lower abdomen, so that they would die in agony.

But those had been blacks.

This obscenity had lain in his arms a few hours before. He had stroked that hair which was matted now with fast congealing blood.

He felt bile flood into his mouth and wanted desperately to vomit.

He heard a movement behind him and he felt the jab of the pistol at the base of his skull.

The man said, "She started to scream."

Murphy backed slowly and the barrel maintained a steady

pressure on his neck. He turned away from the bedroom and heard the door close behind him.

"You bastard," he said.

"Sit down, Murphy." The man in the vest spoke English which was Neapolitan Brooklyn. "My name is Michele and you are my contract. A rushed job and I don't like rushed jobs. My instructions are to persuade you to turn Mr Ragnelli's aeroplane round and to see that it and its contacts are handed back to his agent, who is waiting in Karachi."

"And then?" asked Murphy.

"And then, Mr Murphy, Mr Ragnelli will consider your future with some care."

"And if I can't turn it round?"

"You saw the girl. It was too bad that that should have to happen. And then there is the question of Mr Ragnelli's money, which you appear to have diverted to your own bank." The man sighed deeply. He was talking with a resigned voice like a schoolmaster to an errant pupil.

"You surprise me, Murphy. You were one of Mr Ragnelli's favourites. You were in the upper echelons of the organisation, not like me. I'm just a humble tradesman. And you thought you could get away in Naples of all places. Do you know that I have had a cousin watching your yacht in Ischia for the last twenty-four hours?"

"I can't reach the aeroplane by radio," said Murphy. "It'll be out of range."

"You don't need to. You can telephone. Or cable the captain."

"What do you mean?"

"The aeroplane is on the ground, Murphy. We know that too. That's why I didn't bother to come to your office. I've got cousins everywhere. You'd be surprised how many employees Mr Ragnelli has in this operation. I only wish to know one thing. We can take care of the rest. Just where is that aircraft now?"

*   *   *

It was a small, grubby room with no windows, and the only furniture were two flimsy chairs with rush matting seats and a table with a flower-patterned formica top. The walls were flyblown and a single exposed bulb provided the only light. The room was hot and clammy and the only breatheable air came from a noisy ventilator in the ceiling.

Martin Gore had been sitting in this room for one hour exactly by his wrist chronometer and he was fighting hard against the urge to smash the table and chairs into microscopic fragments against the wall. He was moist with sweat and the ventilator, which badly needed oiling, grated on his already exposed nerves.

"You will wait there while we inspect your flight documents," the blond captain had snarled quite gleefully.

He had been braced for this confinement from the moment that things had started going wrong in mid-air. He had answers for most of the questions they would ask: all right, he was running missiles and not Campbell's tinned soup; he was off course by fifteen hundred miles in a military aircraft with no markings. Weapons were an everyday cargo in this part of the world, sure enough, but the men who flew them were vulnerable.

No, he could have sat in this room for the next twenty-four hours and not murmured a word of protest. He was used to waiting; all pilots are. They wait for weather, for repairs to be carried out, for last minute cargo and delayed passengers. A lot of pilots, like Martin, wait for charters and get hungry.

A cruel resentment was building up inside Martin. It was not the waiting or the discomfort.

In a room, maybe three doors along the corridor outside, he could hear the clatter of china and the clink of expensive glassware. He could smell cooking, good cooking, and he could hear the voice of the French captain and Sorrel's laughter.

He gripped both ends of the table and closed his lips tightly and then said, "Bitch". He said it again several times and it relieved nothing. He experimented with the word. He said, "Perfidious bitch, deceitful bitch," and expanded the thesis, still talking aloud, until he had named the girl a whore, a trollop, a slut, harlot and hooker.

He had never liked the girl from the moment that he and Harry had answered Murphy's advertisement in *Aviation Weekly* and had found themselves facing her in the luxurious Interguns Head Office in Brussels.

Sorrel was typing at the reception desk and her fingers did not stop moving as she glanced up and saw the two men waiting. It was an arrogant, sardonic look.

Harry had muttered, "Man, did you ever feel like you were knee high to a wood-louse? Look at them laser beam eyes."

When she finally condescended to speak to them, there had been something withering and contemptuous about her manner which had them both backing towards the door.

Only Murphy's appearance in the room and his almost immediate offer of the charter from Taiwan saved the situation.

An hour later, when Murphy called the girl into his inner office to dictate to her the terms of his agreement with them, Martin had more time to study her. There was no doubt about it, she was cool and tough and completely self-possessed. When Murphy mentioned the actual fee she interjected, "They're only pilots, you know, not pop stars."

And Martin and Harry liked even less the way she handed the typed-out document and the advance payment cheque with airy condescension.

For all his dislike, though, Martin had built up a strong sexual feeling about the girl. During the days which had followed that first meeting, especially in the loneliness of the Taipei hotel room, he had sets of fantasies about her, each of which ended in the girl surrendering and becoming warm and human.

The sounds of eating and drinking had stopped and the voices in that nearby room were muted. He could not hear laughing any more.

His imagination began to tick like a time-bomb. He saw it all on the dirty wall of the interrogation room as though he were watching a pornographic film. The Frenchman's big, brown, hairy hands were sliding inside that cleavage, her cream white breasts were held and caressed, her cherry pink nipples clutched between nicotine-stained fingers.

"Filth," he said.

And listened. There was no sound now and he strained to hear more, knowing that he was piling on his personal agony.

That bastard's hands were good, blast him. He knew just how to use them on that body. They were deft and gentle and they maintained that steady, ever increasing urgency which he guessed she would like.

It was the Frenchman who was taming her, not Martin.

"Cow."

Martin closed his eyes and turned away from the movie but it went on playing with those hands sliding the zip to the small of her back and she, unprotesting, her tongue too eager for his, allowing him to slide the dress over her buttocks.

"Fornicator!"

Even in the fiercest throes of jealousy, Martin had to smile at the word which had been buried deep in his Church of England past, and he dug for more from the Bible which lurked somewhere in his mind.

"Haridan! Jezebel!"

She was naked now in the film and the Frenchman stood before her and undressed.

"At least you could take that stupid bloody hat off, you Frog bastard," he yelled at the wall. He began to laugh at the fierce scope of his own imagination which suddenly produced horns of the other man's head, sticking out from either side of the *kepi*, and painted a spiky little beard on the face.

The laughter helped to ooze the tension from him for a few moments. He was able to think rationally again. The film had stopped.

And what was she doing? Was she, even now, discarding them, possibly even organising another crew to take Juliet Mike Oscar on? Was she even now talking to Murphy, preparing to leave him and the others in some rat-ridden Arab cell while others took the money?

She was certainly capable of this and so was Murphy. Perhaps he shouldn't have shaken her about in mid-flight. She could be, he was sure, a singularly vindictive person. And yet it was the violence of that encounter which had increased the lust in him for Sorrel. He wanted her very badly.

Then he heard a loud whisper from the other room and the picture show was on again. The two of them were on the bed. Then he saw the fearful dimensions of the Frenchman.

"Oh, no," he said in an appalled voice. "He'll kill her, he'll split her in two."

Martin had picked up the table and was about to use it to smash the door open when he heard a key turning in the lock.

It was a badly fitting key and someone was having trouble. Martin stood and felt his clothes drenched with sweat.

"All right, come in you rapist bastard." He was ready to kill at that moment. He stood crouched, his elbows tucked in, fists bunched like spliced steel.

"Come on, come on, I'm ready."

*   *   *

"I feel it better that you do not burn down the American Consulate."

Alexander Turok was pouring beer for the leader of the Dockers' Union, orange juice for the Secretary of the Somali Unity Front Party and a copious vodka for himself. The three men were sitting on the patio of Turok's villa. It was late afternoon and soon the bright lights of the city would sprawl beneath them.

"Why not?" asked the union leader. "This is an anti-American demonstration you say."

"It is a demonstration against imperialist aggression, not merely by America," said Turok.

"You know more than we do. Just exactly what are we demonstrating against, Consul?"

Turok downed his vodka, put the glass on the table where it had worn a rim over the years, looked up and tapped the side of his nose mysteriously.

"All will be revealed in due course," he said, peering at them through his rheumy eyes. "You have been looking for a demonstration. I assure you that it is an excellent reason."

"Do we attack government offices?"

"The Ministry of the Interior. But stones only. No burning, no looting."

"The British Embassy?"

Turok thought briefly. "No, not yet. Leave the British for the second stage. This is a truly international conspiracy. The British are part of it but they are not the principals."

"Banners. Have we banners?"

"In Arabic, French and English. My staff are preparing them now."

"Press and television?"

"The Tass correspondent will be present and so will all the local stringers. I believe there is a French television crew in Djibouti at this moment. That will ensure good international coverage."

"It is essential that we know why we are calling our men on to the streets," said the Muslim leader. He was a thin-faced man, with the eyes of a fanatic. He clearly did not like Turok or Turok's heavy drinking.

"I can tell you only that this city is in the forefront of a demonstration which will involve every country on the African continent. What is happening must be kept completely secret at this moment. If we show our cards too soon

93

then it may well be that the imperialists will withdraw too early."

"It sounds good," said the docker. "But why can we not attack the American Embassy? You know that my men are anxious to do just that."

"I can only advise you. Stones only. The gendarmes and the légionnaires are spoiling to crack a lot of heads. They would not hesitate to gun down a large number of men at this stage in Djibouti."

Turok offered the vodka bottle to the union leader who shook his head.

"I will telephone you as soon as I have details of the starting time. Be sure to have your group leaders in constant touch from midnight tonight. Now Comrades, thank you for coming here. Please ensure that you are not observed on the way out. Good night, friends."

The two visitors finished their drinks and slipped into the night leaving the Consul alone, staring dispiritedly at the crescent moon which was already bright and clearly visible in the cloudless blue sky. He was gloomy and dyspeptic. He had missed his sleep that afternoon and working in the intense heat in an airless consulate had dehydrated his body.

He emptied the vodka bottle in a quick succession of swallows and went into the living room of the villa where his wife, a small, dowdy woman with a sad, drawn face was mending one of his shirts.

"A busy day?" she asked.

"An urgent job from Moscow. How I hate their urgent jobs. They expect me to have this city alight tomorrow."

"Again?" Her voice was sad and dispirited. Mrs Turok clearly did not like being a consul's wife at any time. She disliked this city more than any in which they had lived.

"Stay indoors tomorrow, woman. Those visitors of mine are too eager. It may get out of hand."

"I wasn't going anywhere. Where is there to go in this awful place? If they burned it down you might get a nice new posting. Somewhere cool like Greenland."

Turok cut a slice of hard brown local bread and smeared

94

it with butter. There were several slices of ham on a covered china dish on the sideboard. He placed the ham on the bread and chewed morosely.

"These Popular Front people can be very tiring. Burn, burn, burn, that's all they can think of. There is every possibility that there will be no American Consulate in this city tomorrow night."

"Didn't they burn that last month?"

"No, that was the West German Legation."

"Oh yes. Poor Mrs Klaus lost all her lovely clothes. She had to miss the British Garden Party."

Turok clipped open a can of German beer. He looked around the room with its shabby furniture and faded family photographs. Almost everything in the room was stained with mildew from the heat and damp. A constant line of red ants made their way from a crack in the wall to the wainscotting below and back again.

"Who would be a consul?" he asked wearily.

"At least no one ever burns down Russian consulates," said Mrs Turok, trying at last to inject a cheerful note into the conversation.

"Pity in a way," he said reflectively. "We could do with a new building. Just imagine, Katya, my wife, air-conditioning like the Americans!" He finished his beer and sandwich and flopped heavily into an armchair.

"It would be too bad if they burnt down the Americans. Consul-General Barker is a good man, the only other decent chess player in Djibouti. And, what's more, he has a very fine stock of bourbon whisky."

*　　*　　*

It was not the captain who entered the interrogation room. The man was stocky and dark-haired and wore a white lightweight suit, a collar and tie and looked cool and unhurried and uncreased as though he had just stepped out from an air-conditioned office. He smiled warmly at Martin and held out his hand. He sniffed around the room with disgust in his face.

"I'm sorry for this," he said. "We cannot seem to be very hospitable. But you must know what airports are like. Luxury for the passengers and squalor for the crews." The man opened the door behind him and left it open.

His voice was slightly high-pitched, almost effeminate. He took a small black document case and placed it on the table. He was a slightly fussy man who did everything with precise movements.

"Sit down, Captain Gore. I hope this will not take long."

"Who are you?"

"My name is Marceau. I am an agent of the Département de Surveillance of this territory."

"A policeman?"

"In a manner of speaking."

"Copper."

The small man smiled thinly.

"I am concerned with your aeroplane and your cargo, Captain," he said. "I have examined your documents and I must tell you that I am much concerned."

"Concerned?"

"For a start, you are carrying weapons."

"We are hardly disguising the fact," said Martin. "The lading bills, consignment notes, the end-user certificate, they are all in order."

Martin was going to like this little man who opened his case and produced a pile of documents and placed them on the table between them.

"All apparently in order. What bewilders me is that your destination is apparently Cyprus, which is north-west of Karachi, whereas you have landed at Djibouti, which is south-west of Karachi. A mild error in navigation, perhaps?"

"We had a fire and lost an engine. We had to jettison fuel."

"You could have diverted to twelve, maybe thirteen different countries. Why this one?"

"I don't think I need to explain. We are an aircraft in transit. As it happens we were instructed to land here. I assumed that there was an engine available."

"You disobeyed an air traffic instruction at Karachi."

"Is that any concern of yours?"

"Not directly, Captain. But it does add a little tarnish to your mission, you must agree."

"Karachi air traffic broke a fundamental rule," said Martin forcefully. "They were yelling at us during an actual take-off. That is unheard of. That's why we didn't turn back and land."

"Who employs you?"

Martin told him. He gave him the whole background from his introduction to Murphy in Brussels to the moment of take-off in Karachi. He played it straight. The questioner nodded occasionally and appeared to be friendly, almost sympathetic.

"Gun-running is not your trade then?"

"I fly people and things from one airfield to another. That's my trade."

"The nature of this load does not worry you?"

"If you mean there are twenty tons of high explosives sitting out there in the sun and surrounded by a lot of heavy-smoking soldiery, yes I am worried. I want to be returned to my aircraft."

"I was talking about the morality of running arms." The Frenchman looked directly into Martin's eyes. There was a mocking look in his own which disconcerted.

"I don't moralise. If I wasn't flying this load, some other man would be. The money is good."

"You are an intelligent man, Captain. That is no answer."

"You mean those things kill people? Is that the morality you mean? But automobiles kill, cigarettes, liquor, asbestos dust, insecticides, so does white bread kill. So if I came in here with a load of Chesterfields and Johnny Walker whisky, what then? Would I still be getting all this morality crap? Like I say, one load is like another."

Marceau took a packet of *Disque Bleu* from his breast

pocket and offered it to Martin, who shook his head. The Frenchman smiled.

"I had hoped for something a little less cynical," he said. "We are a small community and it is always good to talk to new faces."

"Give me a shower and two hours between clean sheets and I'll justify anything you like," said Martin wearily.

The Frenchman suddenly became serious. He talked in a level, calculating tone.

"Captain Gore, please listen carefully. Firstly, I must tell you one of the principal reasons for the delay in my getting to this airport is the fact that I have been talking by telephone to my opposite number in Cyprus. The end-user certificate you have is, in my opinion, entirely bogus. I think that your flight-plan is equally bogus."

Marceau paused and looked at Martin who shrugged his shoulders and said, "Go on."

"I take it that my guess is correct? We will know soon enough."

"Take it any way you like."

"Captain, your true destination if you please."

Martin sighed. The time had come for the mild outrage act, he decided.

"I landed my aircraft here on instructions from the contractor in the honest belief that my crew and myself would be welcomed and that every facility would be given in terms of repair and refuelling."

"I am sure that you will be given every assistance in due course," said the Frenchman. "I merely need to be satisfied that you are acting within the law."

"Which law?"

"Come, come, Captain." The Frenchman wagged an admonishing finger across the table. "Stop playing with words. You are, as they say, a sitting duck. The possession of that forged certificate is enough for me to bring criminal charges against you. So please, answer me this one question. What is your true destination?"

"You seem certain that it is forged."

"I have seen too many of them."

"I'm just a servant," said Martin. "No more than a truck driver delivering a load. Maybe we should send for the boss."

Now the Frenchman sighed deeply.

"Captain, it is hot and stuffy and most unpleasant in this room. Your boss could be several days in arriving. I assure you that we want to see you safely on your way."

"Thank you."

"Now let me make my position clear, finally. The government of this territory has received a cable from the Foreign Ministry in Paris which asks us to give you landing, repair and refuelling facilities. It did not mention that nature of your cargo. Clearly, your employer has some considerable influence in Paris. That does not impress me. The man who signed the cable is known to my department as being a man without a great deal of honour. Now your cargo is going somewhere. I have to establish only that it is not going to enemies of France."

"Whom, for instance?"

"Well, there are the Somalis who have spent years fermenting revolution in this province and who threaten daily to invade. Or there is an entire army of rebels in Chad who are extremely well armed and a constant menace to the population there. And there are many more. I would be failing in my duty if that load were to get into the wrong hands. I need proof, Captain. And once I have that proof I assure you that you will have all the facilities you require as long, naturally enough, as you are able to pay for them."

Martin put his elbows on the table and rested his head in his hands and scratched at his scalp while he thought. "As far as I know the consignee is not an enemy of France. In fact, I think you have done a lot of business with them."

"That is not proof, Captain."

"The freight and the aircraft are destined for Rhodesia,"

said Martin firmly. "You will find a separate set of consignment notes hidden in the airframe."

"I assumed as much." The Frenchman stood up, gathered the papers and put them back in the case. "Thank you, Captain. You are, needless to say, breaking International Law. There is a total embargo on any such delivery to Rhodesia. On the other hand, my government is most reluctant to become involved in a *cause célèbre* and I shall recommend to my minister that we turn a blind eye on this occasion. It is, as I say, too hot."

Martin said weakly, "Thank you."

"But I must tell you at once, Captain, that you will be given a deadline of twelve hours to be out of this territory. My minister is concerned for his own reputation as well as that of France."

"I'll show you the documents."

"I am obliged, Captain," said Marceau quietly. "Had you not done so then we would have had to search your aircraft thoroughly which would have meant removing your load with all the attendant dangers. I think it unlikely that it would have been replaced in the aircraft."

Marceau looked again with keen eyes directly at Martin. The same strange, mocking smile.

"I will tell you why I am allowing you to go, Captain Gore. I sympathise with the Rhodesian cause. Very soon, we French will be booted out of Djibouti. We have brought civilisation to this little state. I dread to think what will happen when it gets into the hands of the Marxists. You can go. It is the people who will fight whom I respect — not you. Be sure to honour your deadline."

*   *   *

They had ridden into the city in an ancient, bone-cracking Citröen cab. Stubbles had been left in the aeroplane, sleeping, while they awaited the new engine.

Martin, who was tired and irritable after the talk with Marceau, flopped in the back seat and said, "Twelve bloody hours. They're asking a hell of a lot from one engineer and a couple of locals who've never seen a Hercules before."

Harry said nothing. He had been unusually quiet and morose from the moment the aircraft had landed and he appeared to have shrunk more and more into himself. The road from the airport was rough and covered in potholes. Martin glanced at Harry. The co-pilot's face appeared to have sagged and gained an unhealthy greyness in its skin texture which had not been there before. He looked old and worried.

Martin squeezed his arm.

"Apart from the fact that we've landed deep in the fertiliser, Harry, my boy, what's worrying you?"

Harry was a long time in answering.

"I guess it's the heat, the smell, I'm just tired."

"It's being back in Africa?"

"Maybe. Maybe it's something like that. I did once swear that I'd never set foot on this birthplace of my ancestors again."

"Just for twenty-four hours. You'll be away from it again tomorrow on a scheduled flight with money waiting at the other end. Come on, cheer up."

Martin was trying hard.

Harry struggled to smile.

"I'm just tired, I guess. And I've been fighting off a premonition about this journey."

"Premonition?" Martin grinned. "I've known you for two whole years now, Harry Black, and you are the most pragmatic, prosaic, feet-on-the-ground flyman I've ever known. You don't wear a St Christopher's medal, you don't carry a mascot. You leave that kind of thing to white men like me. And now you're having premonitions. What the hell sort of premonitions?"

Harry growled the answer.

"Don't bug me, you know what I mean."

"All right, so we've blown an engine. How many times have we blown engines?"

"It's not the engine," said Harry. "It's nothing to do with the fire. Nothing to do with the load. We can get that to Rhodesia without any trouble. It's just a gut feeling about everything else. It's there, like a kind of cancer. It's been there since we signed the contract."

Martin rested his arm behind Harry and felt the engrained dirt on the leather upholstery of the Citröen. The driver gunned the cab mercilessly along the rough road picking up a thick cloud of dust.

Harry continued softly, "You know, brother, every time I took off in Vietnam I reckoned that I'd never land again. That wasn't premonition. That was good, old-fashioned animal fear. This is something else. What about that business in Karachi? And what about that Russian plane? And how about those goons at the airport?"

"There's a logical explanation for all of them," reasoned Martin.

Harry pulled himself up to an upright position and turned to his captain.

"*How* did the Russians know our call sign?"

"They overheard us talking to ground control at Karachi."

"That's crazy and far-fetched and you know it. We were unscheduled if you remember."

"Not at the outset. We began the day as Juliet Mike Oscar."

"I still don't like it."

"It's too hot for paranoia," said Martin sharply. "What's the great phrase in your language? You've got bubbles in your think-tank, Harry my boy. Get some sleep. You'll feel better."

The cab was entering the city. The Sudanese driver held his thumb on the horn ring, scattering goats and chickens which ambled on the main road. A string of worry beads hung from his driving mirror and swayed as he flicked the steering wheel casually, narrowly avoiding parked vehicles. The city was still fast in its siesta. Beggars curled in the shade. The only human life that they saw from the taxi was an idiot who stood in the middle of the road, cackling toothlessly and waving at them with both arms.

The hotel lobby was deserted. Martin had to bang the bell-push several times before the elderly concierge staggered yawning from his cabin at the rear of reception.

When they had signed the registration form the old man took two keys from the rack of pigeon holes behind him. There was a yellow envelope in one of them. He handed it to Martin.

"This came from the airport, Monsieur," he yawned.

Martin opened the envelope. It was a cable signed 'Murphy'. It said, "Await my arrival Djibouti before proceeding."

*   *   *

The hotel room was large and cool with a glistening white marble floor with strips of patterned rush matting on either side of an austere double bed. The heavy wooden shutters were firmly down against the glare of the late afternoon sun. There was a ceiling-high mirror set in exquisitely carved mahogany on one wall and a cooling Utrillo print of Montmartre in the snow on the wall facing it. The room was French Colonial and functional and a big ceiling fan, whirring at sixty revolutions per minute, barely stirred the fetid air.

Martin Gore, naked and still wet from a long, cold shower, sat on the bed and held the receiver of the oldest telephone he had ever seen. It was fashioned from metal and patterned porcelain and it had taken him several minutes to comprehend that he had to press a small red button with his thumb in order to speak to the shrill voiced Arab operator in the administration below. He had woken the operator and she was making the call as difficult as she possibly could for him.

It took almost thirty minutes for him to make contact with

the international operator, but he remained cool and easy tempered. After the nightmare of the interrogation room nothing, he decided, was going to shake him.

He booked a call to Naples. The operator told him that the circuit for Europe did not open until nine o'clock that evening.

"Okay, keep it in please," Martin told the man.

"He replaced the receiver and lay on the bed and gazed up at the stuccoed ceiling and made patterns in his mind from the cracks in it.

He took two cables from the bedside table. They were both from Murphy. The first, which had been delivered to the airport earlier, simply informed them that the engine would be arriving in mid-evening. That was good. Stubbles had a complete ground crew organised to help him replace the damaged engine which had already been removed and crated. The second cable worried him. Just what the hell was Murphy doing? Was it a cash problem? Or was Harry right? Was there some deeper, sinister shadow hanging over this journey?

Sorrel would know, or at least she'd have the kind of intuition which he lacked. But where the hell was she? Since the blue movie show in his mind, Martin had managed to screen Sorrel completely out of his imagination. Marceau knew nothing of the girl. He could only assume that there was a big scene happening somewhere with the blond Frenchman. He had forced himself into not giving a damn about her.

He was still trying hard to force himself when fatigue overtook him and he fell asleep. He had been sleeping for fifteen minutes exactly when the telephone began to ring. He lifted it and, once again, was confused with the red button. He said, "Who's that?" several times and there was no reply. Then he heard a click at the other end.

He turned and went immediately back to sleep.

He was in a deep, profound sleep when there was a loud knocking on the door. He almost fell from the bed and wearily padded across the marble which was pleasantly cool on his feet. He was still naked when he opened it.

It was Marceau who stood in the corridor, still looking elegant and pristine as he had at the airport.

He coughed apologetically and Martin looked down at his own body and smiled.

"I'm sorry," he said. "I was asleep. Come in."

He took a towel from the bathroom and wrapped it round himself.

"What's the trouble?" asked Martin.

"We have trouble, a lot of trouble I think." Marceau looked about the room and then turned to the captain.

"Just who exactly knows what your cargo is, Captain Gore?"

"I've told you everything I know."

"You know the Russians are interested?"

"I had no idea."

"Well, they are. You have brought a load of trouble with you, Mr Gore. I told you it is very hot and I do not want life disturbed in my little province. Telephone calls which I do not like. A great deal of radio traffic which is unusual. My informants tell me of meetings which again I do not like. Captain Gore, just how quickly can you get your new engine fitted and get the hell out of my territory?"

*   *   *

Two hours earlier in Naples a chambermaid, obeying the rule of the hotel, disregarded the 'Do Not Disturb' notice on room 6003 and tapped on the door with her keys. There was no reply. She listened carefully for a few moments and then, still obeying the rules of the hotel, called the house-keeper from the other end of the corridor. The housekeeper, in turn, telephoned the Assistant Manager on the ground floor who gave her permission to accompany the maid into the room.

The two women found James O'Keefe Murphy sitting in

a bedside chair next to the body of the girl. His hands and legs had been tied and his head had been tied into a static position by a thin piece of nylon cord around his forehead and eyes. Twelve of his teeth had been removed and lay on the blood-stained carpet around him.

Murphy had been shot three times in the chest. The Beretta pistol had then been placed in the dead girl's hand and her head had been turned to face her lover.

The screams of the two women shattered the peace of the hotel that afternoon, and the Assistant Manager had spent much of the rest of the day pacifying other hotel residents.

No one had noticed a slender man leave the hotel lobby. Still unnoticed he had made his way to the helicopter landing area above the maritime railway station in Naples and taken a 3,000 lire ticket to the airport where almost immediately he was able to board a domestic Alitalia flight to Rome, where he was fortunate to find a British Airways VC 10 about to board passengers for Cairo.

Even three days later, the Criminal Investigation Department of Naples confided to the press that it was "completely baffled" by the killings at the hotel.

*　　　*　　　*

Only the most practised stranger could decipher the change of mood which came over the city as darkness enveloped it that evening. Those who lived there, whose sixth sense was attuned to the pulse of the city, felt it immediately. It was not yet tension, but there was something ominous about the feeling of expectancy which began to flitter quickly with the night bats from street to street, from suk to suk across teeming Arabtown until every inhabitant was aware of it, but aware only that something was going to happen.

There was nothing tangible, not even the kind of rumour which usually spread like a fast, virulent fever through the city at any time. It was no more than a hint, the first quickening of a pulse. You sensed it in the cries of the beggars, who chanted in an almost imperceptibly higher key, their tempo just marginally faster than normal, and in the absence of laughter in the Arab cafés which were more crowded than usual that evening, the customers talking quietly among themselves with none of the raucousness which usually celebrated the end of the afternoon heat.

The stranger would not notice these things. He would not notice the increase in the clatter of dishes in the hotel kitchen, or the slight tremor in the hands of the waiter who served him, or the unaccustomed loudness of the voices of the légionnaire officers at the corner table.

They knew that something was afoot in the city that evening. They assumed that it had to do with the unwelcome visitors at the airport, but at that time they knew only that something was wrong with the normal rhythm of the city, that something was going to happen.

At exactly seven o'clock local time that evening, after a slow and uneventful flight down the length of the Red Sea, a Super Constellation of Arab Airways landed at Djibouti Airport. There were twenty-one passengers, who included a French diplomat and his family who had been on leave in Brittany, several Arabs on a pilgrimage to Mecca, three Nestorian nuns and a relief Air France crew. The twenty-first passenger, who had joined the flight at the very last minute in Cairo, was thin and well tanned and wore a white golfing jacket and blue jeans.

He was questioned for several minutes by the immigration officers in the airport building. They were anxious to know why he did not have any baggage. He explained in poor French with a heavy Italian accent, and with frequent and angry gesticulation, that his suitcases had been mislaid in transit between airlines.

The immigration desk examined his passport with considerable care and finally satisfied themselves that he was, indeed, Michele Vincento, aged thirty, a ventilation engineer of Naples who was in possession of more than enough money in lire and francs not to become a burden on the territory. They stamped his passport with a seven-day temporary visa and allowed him in to Djibouti on condition that he reported to the Préfecture twice daily.

One hour later, stopping at a small general store in the city centre where he bought a shirt, some socks, toiletries and a kitchen knife, together with a cheap plastic suitcase, Vincento checked into the hotel Charles de Gaulle and was being ushered to a room three doors away from the room in which Martin Gore was sleeping.

It was only when he undressed for a shower that he noticed his vest was heavily smeared with blood.

|| || ||

As Alexander Turok snored and sweated and turned continually in an uneasy, trouble-filled and drunken sleep, the leader of the Somali United Front Party was addressing a meeting of his committee in a small house in the centre of the city. The committee room was lit only by a candle which added to the conspiratorial atmosphere. "I have talked to the drunken Russian," said the secretary. "He makes no sense, as usual. Something is happening and if we wait for him we would be losing a major opportunity for a great demonstration. He would have us wait. I do not trust him."

"What do we demonstrate against?" asked a committee member.

"It is that which I want to know."

"The city seethes with rumours about an aircraft which arrived today. The army has surrounded it. The pilot is under arrest."

"What kind of aircraft?"

"A big American transport."

"Military?"

"It would appear thus."

"An American military aircraft," mused the secretary. "That would appear to be justification enough. The men are ready?"

"And the weapons."

*　　*　　*

Martin was wakened from a deep sleep by the sound of breathing close to his face. He turned quickly, ready to spring. Immediately he felt the soft warmth of a woman's body. He leaned over and switched on the bedside light. Sorrel was sitting on the side of his bed.

She was wide awake, wearing a demure, virginal white nightdress.

She said, "Hi."

He rolled over and looked at the fan turning slowly above him.

"Jesus Christ," he said. "I would have thought you would have had enough today."

"Take that hate out of your voice," said Sorrel softly. "I didn't get laid, if that's what you mean."

"That's what I meant. What were you doing?"

"Getting you a twelve-hour stay."

"And you're telling me that that Frenchman didn't?"

"He couldn't."

Sorrel held up her hand and let her little finger droop.

"He blamed it on the heat," she said, and giggled.

Martin was wide awake now. He looked at his wristwatch.

"Don't you realise that we need sleep, all of us? Just what do you want?"

"I wanted to talk to you while the other two weren't here."

Martin eyed her suspiciously. "I think they should be here," he said. "If you're playing a game of divide and conquer, darling, forget it."

Her breasts were clearly outlined through the thin fabric

of the nightdress. Even in that surprised state, Martin found himself wanting her. Her eyes continued to mock him.

She held up her arm. There was a blackening bruise where Martin's hand had clenched it earlier.

"You don't like me one little bit, do you," she said. It was a statement.

"What a time to start this kind of thing," he said. "I don't like the way you look at me. I don't like the contempt in your face."

"I'm sorry," she said. "I never intended contempt."

"You certainly delivered it," said Martin. He was wary, not sure of what was coming next.

"I'm sorry," she said in a direct tone.

He realised suddenly that she meant it.

"It's just that it's the way I look at men," she said. "It keeps them at a distance. There's no involvement. I've had bad experiences of men."

Martin remained entirely on his guard. He knew he had to keep her at arm's length. But he was finding it more and more difficult to stifle the urge to pull her under the thin coverlet which concealed his nakedness.

"It's very easy to misread people," he said.

"I read you very well," said Sorrel, looking directly into his eyes. "You've had a bad experience with women or a woman, haven't you?"

"Two years ago, yes."

"Who was she?"

"A woman. She came into my life and we fell very much in love."

"You miss her?"

"Sometimes, very much. Look," he said. There was exasperation in his voice. "Why have you come to this room? What have you come to say?"

"I came to say that there's a full security alert at the airport and it's everything to do with our aeroplane. That much I did learn from the Foreign Legion."

"So what can we do about it now?"

"I just thought you ought to know. You the captain."

"For Christ's sake, Sorrel. Sleep is more important at this moment. What else did you want?"

"To get laid," she said softly and began to take off the nightdress.

Later, Martin leaned over Sorrel who was just about to fall asleep. He took Murphy's telegram from the table on the other side of the bed and showed it to her.

She read it and smiled. "So Murphy's coming here," she said. "You cunning, English sonofabitch. You waited."

"What does it mean?" asked Martin.

"I think it means that we're in big trouble," she said.

$$*\qquad*\qquad*$$

In a similar room four doors down the hotel corridor, Harry Black found it impossible to sleep. The ceiling fan in his room did not work and he lay, his face glistening with sweat, and listened to the street noises outside. His body was pained with tiredness but his mind was infuriatingly active.

He was tortured by a string of doubts about the whole enterprise, and he was aware now of the taunting conscience.

The money had been too good to turn down. He had not cared, he did not particularly care now, what happened to the weapons.

But he *was* a black man.

Harry Black, gun-running for whitey.

So what, he said to himself, I'm no racialist. I've taken more shit from my black brothers than I ever did from the white man.

Whitey made me a major and they gave me good money and aeroplanes to fly. It was a black airline that fired me because the passengers wanted white pilots, a black dictator who threw me into prison and black warders who kicked me about. A black landlord who foreclosed on my old man.

Here was the conscience.

No, George Washington Black, good and Godly citizen of Houston, Texas, he wouldn't approve of his son carrying guns for the crackers. George Washington Black, retired now, a champion of the Civil Rights movement, a lay preacher, a man with a fierce pride in his only son.

Harold Black, Major, USAF, AFC.

Who was humping enough weaponry to bury half the black population of southern Africa, his cousins indeed.

He, Harry Black, little Harry who had walked between the lines of paratroopers to school, his chin thrust out, blood streaming from a head cut, while white kids jeered and hurled rocks and bottles at him and the others.

He, the great-grandson of a slave, carrying the white man's shit.

For money. For Martin Gore.

For him, you'd do almost anything. He sprang you from the jail and brought you away from that madman and he looked after you, nursed you, fed you, got you this job, got you enough money to get home, see the Old Man right.

Now he's crazy, that Martin. He's committing treason and he knows it, and you, Harry, you're committing ethnic suicide. Can't you see it in the papers now? Except, who cares, man?

He said it aloud.

"Who cares? Who gives a monkey's left tit?"

A voice, cold and void of any emotion, spoke in the silence of Harry's room.

"Mr Ragnelli cares."

The light at Harry's bedside flicked on. Vincenzo knelt by his bedside. He held a long kitchen knife at a point immediately over Harry's carotid artery. Harry saw the man only from the corner of his eyes.

"Hallo, black man," said Vincenzo. "One tiny move and you'll be dead in five seconds."

The other man was grinning. Harry felt the prick of the knife point and lay very still.

"Black man, I promise you it's nothing personal. Indeed,

tell you, I'll make a deal. I can make this last a very long time like with Murphy. Very noisy before he went through the exit, your boss Murphy. Just tell me where the girl is and you won't feel a thing."

Harry said, "Murphy's dead?"

"Affirmative, Mr Black. Very dead. I hate to tell you but you're all going to die. I have signed an agreement to that effect."

"Why, man?" asked Harry weakly.

"Where's the girl?"

"How would I know?" said Harry. He felt the pressure of the knife increase.

It was at that moment that the first of ten bombs planted by the Somali United Front Party exploded under a parked car in a street six blocks away. The noise was enough to deflect Vincenzo's attention and allow Harry to convulse himself away from the knife and off the bed.

He was naked, supremely vulnerable.

Vincenzo leapt on to the bed and stood on it for a second, the knife poised like a matador's sword. He was still grinning when he stepped towards Harry.

Harry was ready this time. Breaking all the rules of unarmed combat he moved towards the Italian, reaching out for the knife hand. He felt a sharp sting and heard the blade grating along the bones of his right hand. His weight and power and rage carried Vincenzo against the wall.

Harry brought his knee hard into the other man's groin and crashed the top of his head against Vincenzo's nose.

As the killer sagged and began to slide down the wall, Harry grabbed at his throat with his good hand and strangled him.

*   *   *

Martin was woken for the fifth time that night, this time by a frantic hammering on the hotel room door. He opened it to find Harry, swaying drunkenly, a sickly, ridiculous grin on his face. Martin's first instinct was one of fury, but then the co-pilot held up his hand. "It's okay, Martin." He could barely whisper. "It's my right hand. I can still fly on my left."

He fell forward and Martin grabbed him by the shoulders. Sorrel was awake now and helped him to lay Harry on the bed. Blood was fountaining from the cut making an irregular set of splashes on the marble floor.

"He'll need stitches," said Martin.

"Stitches?" said Sorrel. "Don't you see how deep that cut is, Martin? He'll need major surgery."

She was prodding Harry's arm in search of the artery when there was a massive explosion in the street outside. The windows in the room appeared to bulge inwards and then they, too, exploded into a million fragments. For a fraction of a second it seemed that the floor was upended. Martin and Sorrel were hurled across the room and crashed through the open doorway. They came to, seconds later, lying on a carpet of glass fragments.

*   *   *

Turok heard the bomb from several miles away. He woke and walked unsteadily to the verandah of his house.

As he watched, another bomb flashed from the direction of the docks. The 'crump' of the explosion followed a few seconds later. He heard the clatter of machine gun fire and the blast of smaller explosions.

"Fools," he shouted. "Ungrateful fools. They should have waited for the signal. Moscow will have me shot."

He heard his wife say from behind him, "Come to bed, Alexander Alexandrovitch, there is nothing you can do. They cannot punish you more than they have punished you by sending you to this terrible place."

The Consul-General shrugged his shoulders in agreement and followed her into the bedroom.

*   *   *

Fifteen hundred miles to the south on the apron of the small airport at Mocímboa-da-Praia, Major Yefgeni Uglov sweltered in his silver 'G' suit by the fuselage of an orange painted MIG 21 UTI fighter and quietly cursed Africa. The mercury fuel cell which powered the air-conditioning inside the suit had failed and the nearest replacement was a thousand miles to the south in Beira. The rubbery plastic clung to his body making each movement an agony of discomfort. The suit itself was optional wear. He could have flown in shirt and slacks, except that the aircraft was still inhabited by red ants from the practical joke of the previous week. They appeared from all parts of the fuselage and engine housing. The only protection was to seal himself completely. He preferred this to the fierce agony of their bites.

The local bowser crew had succeeded in spilling several gallons of kerosene at the last refuelling and the stench drove him from the only available shade under the razor-edged delta wing. His morning mood of sadness and disillusion with this continent had returned. Africa, he decided, should be left to Africans. They deserved it. It deserved them.

It deserved, certainly, this one particular cursed fly which had been plaguing him for the past half hour. It had settled on his cheek earlier and he had slapped at it so savagely that he had loosened one of the stainless steel fillings in his teeth. His morale was always at its lowest ebb at that time in Africa and on this particular day it had never been lower.

Earlier Uglov had been decidedly cheerful as he left the Ambassador's office. The signal from Moscow meant that he was in action again for the first time since, clad in the uniform of a Lieutenant in the Egyptian Air Force, he had led his squadron of MIG 23s against Israeli tanks in the Sinai Desert.

The message had specified exactly how the operation would be conducted. A Mozambique pilot would take the actual credit; he, Uglov, sitting in the rear seat, would ensure that the black man did not become too exuberant and destroy the C 130. Indeed, Uglov had made up his mind that he would conduct the entire operation with the African as a passenger only.

He worked at the maximum speed in near impossible conditions that morning in the belief that his target was airborne and would be overhead in a matter of a few hours.

His pilots, in their keenness, had used the entire quota of the SB 06 air-to-air missiles several days before; and his intention now had been to convert two actual missiles which were fully armed and heavily packed with high explosive into weapons which would create a relatively small explosion at a distance which he judged to be 'safe-dangerous'. It was a task which would have dismayed the finest armourer, and Uglov was without any advice or expert assistance except for the air force signal from Moscow.

The work had involved taking and clamping the ten foot long cylinder on to a workbench with a makeshift vice; and then, using a massive wrench and aided only by a Mozambiquan mechanic, applying all his strength to unscrew and remove the globular aluminium head.

The first two feet of the missile were taken up by the infra-red guidance system, an entire miniature computer, the size of a large thermos flask, which had the capacity to seek and find the heat of an aircraft exhaust within a radius of three miles. This was relatively simple for Uglov to remove. The complex assembly was placed on the workbench. The problem now was to remove the high explosive inside.

It was when he placed the small inspection light into the metal cavity that he saw just how impossible the rest of the job was. The steering engine unit was made up of four electric motors, each of them operating independently and controlling the angles of the four shark fin-like steering vanes. They were obviously impossible to remove in the short time allotted to him.

He had stared for a long time at the confusion of machinery. Behind this, he knew, was a bulkhead which removed to expose four long cotton padded tubes of melinite, each primed with an individual fail-proof detonator. He looked at his wrist watch and made a decision which, he knew, might well cost him his life.

Using a watchmakers' lens and a minute screwdriver, he carefully adjusted the mechanism of the close proximity detonator unit in the rear of the guidance system to ensure that the missile would explode at the maximum possible distance from the target. In this way he could be sure of damaging the transport but, unless he could get in a perfect shot at the subsonic speed required, there was an excellent chance of the blast crippling, probably destroying his own aircraft at the same time.

The missiles were then carefully clipped into their pods beneath each wing and their launching systems checked.

The secondary armament system on the MIG were two NR 30 mm cannons in either wing. Methodically, Uglov defused each of the forty shells in each ammunition belt. At least, he reasoned, he could puncture the fuel tanks on the target without starting a fire.

Finally, with a cynical prudence, Uglov had disconnected all firing systems in the front cockpit. Umboto, the pilot he had selected for the mission, was excitable and almost certainly would not understand the subtlety of the manoeuvre they were attempting.

The tall Mozambiquan pilot had almost danced with delight at the briefing. Uglov had to physically restrain him from calling his relatives.

Soon after 11.00 am that morning they had taken off from the Beira base and flown at supersonic speed to Mocímboa, only to receive word that their target had been delayed. They were to remain on standby.

Umboto had disappeared. He had last been seen striding happily across the tarmac in search of a new conquest in a strange town.

Uglov stood and cursed his pupil and Africa even more fluently. His suit clung to his naked body. The control tower at Mocímboa was not able to relay messages on the military frequency. He was forced to stand on the concrete griddle and wait, listening to the crackle in the receiver in the MIG for the latest word from the Embassy.

He was composing another sad letter to his wife in his mind when he heard his call sign being shouted.

"Volley. Volley. Stand down for six hours. Report by land line."

Uglov climbed up to the cockpit and switched off the receiver. He pulled the master power switch to 'off'. He slid the canopy closed and began the long, uncomfortable walk, his suit sloshing around him, across the airfield to the control tower.

*   *   *

The letter was headed FROM THE DESK OF GENERAL GEORGE SAUNDERS and it was typed on an IBM 3,000 typewriter which printed in the familiar Pentagon type. It was addressed to Group Captain Michael Borrison, DSO, DFC, Royal Rhodesian Air Force, and it read:

My dear Mike,

I want to introduce you to Harry Black, one of the best flyers the US Air Force ever had, who will be delivering a consignment to you. He is by far the most outstanding CHARLIE ONE-THIRTY flyer we have available at the moment and he has a truly remarkable Special Service record. I feel that his experience in Uganda may be of special interest to you, especially in view of his color. Don't forget that I am due to remove a few bucks from you on the golf course when we get together here in June. I am enclosing six Dunlop 65s with the load — I gather they are hard to come by in your neck of the woods.

With best wishes,
George.

Natalia Rogov held the letter which was contained between two sheets of glass and turned to Litvinoff.

"Explain, please."

"When you set out to deceive it is best to do it with absolute thoroughness," said her uncle. "There are more."

He indicated the pile of documents on a table by the window in his office.

"The letter you hold simply indicates the connection between the Pentagon and the rebel government in Rhodesia. It will be found in Black's briefcase. We know that the typewriter in General Saunders' office has certain minute irregularities and we have reproduced them in our workshops. We also have a set of the General's fingerprints and they will be attached to the letter. An independent forensic expert will open this letter and examine the contents. That has been arranged."

"What else?"

"Various items which will be essential for the world's press. A letter from Interguns Incorporated which also implicates the State Department. A love-letter from the girl Francis to her boss Murphy typed on the Interguns typewriter which once again is easily identifiable. That will tell us a great deal about Gore and his Secret Service associations.

"All forged?"

"But, of course."

"I agree you are being very thorough," said Natalia. "But might you not be adding too much dressing to salad? Surely the weapons themselves are sufficient."

Litvinoff laughed. He put his arms around his niece and clutched her shoulder with a giant hand.

"This is an exercise in propaganda, Natalia my innocent," he said. "The great reading public delights in minutiae like this. An aeroplane full of hardware, so what? It will be forgotten in a day or so. But build up a conspiracy and then unfold it piece by piece, letter by letter, a little romance, an indiscretion here and there, that's what they will have for days on end. Just look at this."

Litvinoff picked up a small blue book from the table.

"A deposit account in the name of Martin Gore at the National Westminster Bank, Town Hall Branch, 103 Church Road, Hove, Sussex. See — a regular payment of £150 has been paid into his account on the first day of each month from Barclays Bank, London Road, Uxbridge, Middlesex since July, 1969, the date of his discharge."

"Meaning?"

"The RAF pay office used that branch of Barclays Bank."

"But surely they will deny this immediately?"

"Not immediately. Gore has an actual account at that bank in Hove. It will be several days before the bank will be prepared to make any statement about a customer's account. By then the world will be content in the knowledge that Martin Gore is still in the pay of the British Government."

Natalia looked worrked. "I still think the dressing is too thick. The arms in that aeroplane are the important item. They will be forgotten in this Agatha Christie charade. I have a feeling that this will rebound on you."

Litvinoff threw the bank book on to the desk in front of them. His voice barely concealed impatience.

"This charade, as you call it, will be on a TU 144 to Mozambique tonight," he said. "I am waiting at the moment for one more document which, you will be shocked to learn, is a letter from Cyrus Vance to the head of the Mafia in New York."

Natalia was instantly furious.

"How insane can you become in this office?" she shouted. "Even if such a document existed, it would never be carried on that aeroplane. You're crazy."

"Of course it will not be found in the aircraft, silly child." Litvinoff beamed with delight. "It will be found in a garbage can, turn into four pieces and slightly charred. The garbage can will also contain remains of incinerated trash and will be outside Frank Ragnelli's apartment in 59th Street, New York City, exactly twenty-four hours after the first major denial of complicity by the State Department."

Litvinoff continued to smile.

"You like it?"

"It's ridiculous," stormed Natalia. "Just who is going to grub through the trash cans of Central Park South?"

"Comrade niece, you forget that the biggest growth industry in the United States is investigative journalism. The press would be delighted with such a document. The fact that it was found in a trash can adds, I assure you, to its authenticity."

The big man failed to notice the look of disgust on his niece's face.

"It will not be believed," she said.

"It will, especially when you produce it at the United Nations together with the rest of the collected evidence."

"When I produce it?" Natalia's eyes were wide open with disbelief and shock.

"I must tell you, Natalia, that you have just been appointed the principal advocate for the prosecution. It was your idea. We have added, as you say, the dressing. You leave for New York tomorrow."

*   *   *

Marceau sat in the ambulance which took them, its sirens howling, through the darkened streets of the city to the airport. One explosion had destroyed the electricity generator allowing thousands of demonstrators to roam the streets, shattering windows and hurling stones at police and légionnaires with impunity.

"What did I tell you?" he yelled. "The whole city will be ablaze by dawn. I want you out of here, you understand?"

The agent clutched a radio transceiver in his hand. There was a continual chatter in excited French.

Harry was lying on the stretcher, his hand heavily bandaged. Sorrel was stroking his head with a piece of lint soaked in eau-de-cologne. Martin sat grim-faced and looked at his co-pilot.

They heard the noisy crashing of stones against the side of the ambulance. Then a shot and the sound of the bullet ricocheting from the roof.

"Get down!" shouted Marceau. "We have reached the airport."

They climbed directly from the ambulance into the waiting Hercules. The aircraft was completely ringed with jeeps and machine guns now and they could hear the yelling of demonstrators in the darkness beyond.

Stubbles was waiting on the flight-deck. His clothes were smeared with oil and grease. He blinked at the sight of Harry.

"Holy Cow, Skipper," he said. "What in hell happened to him?"

"I'll tell you. Can we get this aircraft off the ground?"

"The engine was fixed fifteen minutes ago. I've tested it as best I can. I've got my fingers crossed."

"Help me get Harry into the bunk. Can you co-pilot?"

"I'll try, Captain. What's the big occasion?"

"Get in that seat and start the checks," said Martin urgently. "Sorrel, strap Harry in, leave him and sit in Stubbles' seat and do as he tells you."

"You're joking," she said.

There was a series of violent explosions from the perimeter of the airport.

"Close the main door and do as I tell you," he shouted. He saw Marceau standing at the foot of the steps.

"Is this a fast enough turn round for you?" he asked. His voice was heavy with sarcasm and irony.

"I apologise that you had to rush, Captain," said the Frenchman. "I would have liked to have talked to you some more."

Marceau held up his hand and Martin shook it.

The Frenchman said, "Take care, Captain. I don't think your troubles are over yet."

Ten minutes later Juliet Mike Oscar was cleared for take-off by Djibouti control. As she hurtled down the runway, Martin saw a crowd of robed figures standing at the end of the runway, waving banners and hurling rocks at the aircraft's landing lights.

The soft, fat, low-pressure tyres missed the nearest of them by inches.

As they flew safely out to sea, Martin looked back through the side panel. Several buildings in Djibouti were well ablaze. He saw further bomb flashes.

He wondered more and more about the sequence of events which had overtaken them, wondered about the Russian jet which had trailed them on the first leg, and wondered finally just exactly what Marceau had meant about 'more trouble'.

*　　　*　　　*

At the age of thirty-six, Yefgeni Uglov was, in almost every sense, an outstanding product of the Soviet revolution. He was an entirely dedicated member of the Communist Party who could recite lengthy excerpts from the writings of Marx, Engels and Lenin. He was immensely proud of his diplomas in each of these subjects from the Red Air Force Academy. His record as a pilot was impeccable; he flew his aircraft exactly as the Mikoyan handbook dictated he should fly them and flew also in the unerring belief that no Soviet-built aircraft could ever flame-out or suffer an hydraulic failure or any of the myriad misfortunes which overtook the aircraft of other nations.

Uglov was a man of culture whose vacations in Moscow and Leningrad were spent slavishly following art collections, symphony concerts, poetry readings and the ballet.

His morals were completely irreproachable. He remained faithful to his beloved Natasha throughout his lengthy absences abroad and scarcely looked at another woman at any time.

He applied an equal fanaticism to his health. From the moment that, as a fresh-faced schoolboy, he had sworn his oath of allegiance to the Party and to Mother Russia, Yefgeni Uglov had never touched alcohol in any form and the very smell of tobacco made him decidedly queasy. He spent an hour of each morning performing rigorous gymnastics and the embassy doctor, perhaps with an overtone of cynicism in his voice, had recently declared him "a perfect specimen of Soviet manhood".

Only one factor in his make-up had precluded him from a lifting us a component. The truth was that he had absolutely no sense of humour.

When all these component parts of Yefgeni Uglov's make-up were put together it became doubly surprising that an African dawn should find him staring at the rush matting roof of a mud hut in Mocímboa with a fierce and agonising pain which throbbed remorselessly and continuously behind his eyes. It was a pain which he had never known before. A pain so intense that he dared not move his head and lay still for fifteen minutes as he tried desperately to organise his mind and to establish who he was, where he was and why he was there.

His first vague opinion was that he must have been in an accident. Slowly, his nervous system began to co-ordinate with his brain, and he realised that it was the whole of his body which hurt.

Each limb shot a different kind of electricity which made him want to convulse. His mouth was arid and dry and the few functioning taste buds on his tongue recorded a foulness which he had never before experienced. He whimpered a little and said "oh no" several times.

It was only then that the terrible realisation came over him of just why he was here. The mortifying pain was enjoined with wave after wave of shame and self-disgust.

There was a rasping sound close to him. He mustered courage and closed his eyes and turned his head slowly to the right and heard the straw in the mattress crackle like cannon fire in his mind. He opened his eyes, dreading what he was going to see.

There was a woman on the mattress next to him. She was young and her chubby face was relaxed in a smiling sleep. Her mouth was slightly open and she snored quietly and rhythmically. A fly had settled on the end of her nose. There was a trickle of greenish-coloured saliva running from her mouth to a point just below a cheap plastic ear-ring. Uglov moaned a little and then he suppressed the moan for fear of waking her up.

He felt a movement on the other side of his body. He closed his eyes again and braced himself to turn. There was another woman lying there. His face was no more than an inch from a pair of large balloon-like breasts which trembled slightly as she breathed. The big nipple nearest him had been rouged and he stared at it hypnotised, his eyes fixed with terror upon its grossness.

He whispered "oh no" again and stared back up at the matting in horror. The sun was dappling through the roof, its brightness causing a new sensation of physical pain to him, but the pain was nothing to the feeling which engulfed him.

It was only then that the truth flooded in to his brain, the true and terrible realisation poured out from his memory lobes in an ugly, fearful torrent.

It had been that pilot Umboto, curse him.

"Come, good Major, come and meet the real people of my country," he had said. "You don't want to spend the night in a lonely hotel, not by yourself. No, no, just for thirty minutes. You come, eh?"

More from fear of being reported to the Embassy for his anti-social ways, he had accepted the invitation with a repugnant reluctance.

There had been an underground discotheque, he remembered that; and he remembered the curious taste of the iced orange juice which he had demanded, and the sudden sense of well-being which it had induced in him. He remembered dark bodies whirling around him in the electronic flicker. He remembered beginning to relax, beginning to laugh at Umboto's wild antics. And he remembered being crushed against a massive black girl whose body appeared to envelope him.

He remembered a bar where he drank more orange juice, and the women who had trooped in and surrounded him while Umboto encouraged them to grasp and paw at his body.

And then this place.

He raised his head slowly and with difficulty. The women were both naked. He shuddered as he remembered how he had coated them both with palm oil, how he had actually laughed as they drenched his body in the same foul, musty smelling fluid. And all three had slithered over and under each other, his teeth snapping for their jiggling breasts, his head disappearing into every kind of recess.

"Oh no," he murmured.

The room still reeked of that oil and their bodies. No, it could not have happened to him.

He put his hands slowly down on his own body and found that that too was naked. He touched his groin and felt a painful tenderness that he had never felt before. Oh no, it could not have been him who had mounted them both, who had charged at the fat one like a prize bull, singing all the time the anthem of the Red Air Force at the top of his drunken voice.

The Red Air Force. Was he not a Major in the Red Air Force? Umboto was sure to tell. He would be disgraced. He would be called before the Ambassador and then flown home to Moscow to face a court martial. Perhaps not. His pilot colleagues had behaved equally disgracefully in many parts of the world and many of them had been promoted. But how could he, Yefgeni Uglov, moralist and socialist, gain the respect of his trainee African pilots after this?

And oh, no, he was flying a mission on this very morning.

With consummate effort and more, much more discomfort, he raised his head again, averting his eyes from the dusky bodies which lay parallel with his. He saw his shirt and trousers hanging from one wall of the hut. He climbed out from between the two women, taking enormous care not to disturb them. Each movement was such that he wanted to collapse back on to the mattress and go back to sleep or to close his tortured eyes at least.

He was on his feet now. He staggered slightly but just managed to stay upright. He turned and faced the women and the sight of their rounded fleshy bodies made him want to retch. He stifled the vomit and began to dress.

The shirt was relatively easy, and he was able to get into his trousers and sighed with relief that he was no longer naked in this obscene presence. He stumbled several times as he tried to put on his socks and finally gave up and slid his naked feet into the shoes on the floor. He checked his wallet, which was untouched. Then he took ten Mozambique escudos from it and jammed them over a nail in the mud wall.

He had to bend low to get through the doorway and as he did he heard a movement from the bed. The fatter of the two women was sitting up. She was scratching her breasts vigorously and all her glistening teeth showed in a huge grin.

"Okay, baby," she said. "You no want more fucky-fucky? You good man, eh, give plenty fucky."

Uglov fell out of the entrance of the hut and pulled himself up from the earth outside to see Umboto, fully dressed, crawling from another hut. He was zipping up the fly of his trousers.

"Good morning, good Major," said the trainee pilot. "I hope you enjoyed my cousins."

*　　　*　　　*

From the moment she had rounded Cape Guardafini on the far north-eastern tip of the hostile Somali Republic, her crew taking scrupulous care to avoid transgressing any territorial limits, Juliet Mike Oscar began to climb slowly to her ceiling as the auto pilot drove her southwards. As they flew an almost parallel course with the distant, khaki-coloured coast, the four Allisons, even though the propellers were set at the most economical pitch, began to make a definite impression on the fuel gauges, and the lighter the fuel load the more she climbed, until the altimeter needle slipped past the thirty thousand feet mark.

Stubbles sat in the co-pilot's seat, occasionally leaning dramatically back to check his own engineer's instruments. Apart from a few minor adjustments of the trim tabs and the noting of a few odd pieces of data in the logbook there was little for him to do except monitor the local frequencies and to check the aircraft's course.

Harry lay in the bunk, still fully clothed, his right hand heavily bandaged. Martin had ordered him to rest. There was an unhealthy grey sheen on the co-pilot's face. He took occasional gulps from an emergency oxygen mask and Sorrel, who had been left in charge of him, was gratified to see his colour begin to improve and some sparkle in his eyes.

Thirty minutes earlier Martin had disappeared from the flight-deck into the depths of the cargo hold. He had given no reason. He had said to her, "Make sure Harry stays resting. He's lost a hell of a lot of blood. The thing is I can't possibly land this plane without that left hand of his."

The flight droned on. Harry finally slept. It was a short sleep lasting no more than fifteen minutes but he was smiling when he woke. Automatically he tried to heave himself off the bunk but Sorrel held him down.

"Captain says you're to rest," she said firmly.

"Where is he?" said Harry. His voice which had been weak was much stronger now.

"Search me," said Sorrel. "He can't have gone far, that's for sure. You just lie there, still."

"I'm hungry," he said.

"Well, they say that's a good sign. There's some soup in one of the flasks. Stay there and I'll get you some."

She spoon-fed the co-pilot, cradling his head in her left hand.

Between mouthfuls he said, "Tell me, Miss Francis . . ."

"You know my first name, Harry," she said.

"Oh, so we're all buddy buddies now," Harry chuckled.

"You could say we'd reached an understanding," she said quietly.

"Honey, it's good of you to look after me but I've got to tell you I still don't trust you."

"You don't have to. The captain does, that's all that matters."

"He's a trusting sort of guy."

Sorrel spooned more soup into Harry's mouth.

"You're real fond of him, aren't you?" she said.

"He saved my life."

"How?"

"It's a long story, baby, and a lot of it ain't for tellin' to young ladies. You see, our illustrious employer Idi Amin Dada decided that me and Martin were working for the Israelis. He had us both thrown into his prize prison. Now the British Government did some powerful ass licking and Martin was sprung. The State Department weren't going to play ball, even for an Air Force Cross holding American citizen, and I was held. Do you know, that guy came back for me, helped me break out and got me out of Uganda. He's a brave man. That's why I don't want him hurt."

"Why should he be hurt?" she asked.

"Because, honey child, I've got a powerful sort of gut feeling that you would happily slice three throats in this aeroplane if you could see a buck in it. You're a hard lady."

For a moment he expected her to throw the rest of the soup in his face.

"Of course I'm hard," she snapped. "I'm a one hundred

per cent tempered nickel-steel bitch. And if you want to know something else, Major Black, I don't like niggers."

"Oh," said Harry, smiling broadly. "You, too?"

"They teach you not to like black men in Barberton, Ohio. It's a hard-working town where jobs are hard to find and a girl learns that she's got to survive somehow."

The tension between them was eased by the slam of the cargo hold hatch closing. Martin emerged and came up on to the flight-deck. His shirt and hands were covered in grease and he was cleaning himself on a piece of cotton waste. He looked at the two of them.

"Well, well," he said. "Lazarus has risen. I was reckoning that we would have to bury you at sea."

The captain leaned forward athletically over Stubbles' shoulder and read the fuel gauges. He sat in the engineer's seat and changed the fuel flow from the outer to inner wing tanks and glanced through the side panels at the four engines. He patted Stubbles playfully on the back and turned back to Sorrel.

"We'll be crossing the Equator in ten minutes," he shouted. "Maybe we should have some sort of party."

She gave Harry the last spoonful of soup. She took the plastic container and spoon and put them back in the supply cupboard.

She turned to Harry and said, "Now get some more sleep."

*   *   *

"This is All Kenya Radio broadcasting on short wave. Here is the news. The possibility that the rebel government of Rhodesia will surrender to the weight of African opinion increased today during talks between an envoy of Britain and the Prime Minister of South Africa, Dr Vorster. Mr Ian Smith, the leader of the illegal right-wing racist government of Rhodesia, is expected to meet with the British envoy at some time today or tomorrow."

The broadcast was being relayed through the intercom system of Juliet Mike Oscar. They all heard it.

Martin said, "That's all we need. Trust that bastard. He's been a traitor for the last eight years and now he's stabbing *us* in the back." He smiled wryly.

The announcer continued. "During serious rioting in the French occupied territory of Djibouti last night more than forty people, mostly Arabs, were killed by French forces. The cause of the rioting is not known but a spokesman for the Progressive Front in Djibouti said that a spontaneous demonstration of anti-Colonial feeling had been put down in the most brutal way."

Martin switched the radio off.

"Well at least there's not an all stations alert for us," he said.

*   *   *

They were now two hours south of the Equator and heading south by south west, the Kenyan and Tanzanian coastline well to the west, their course taking them directly into the Mozambique Channel. Harry slept and Stubbles dozed. Sorrel sat in the co-pilot's seat, her eyes shut. Martin stayed awake, keeping a careful watch on all of them; although he knew that what he was doing was deliberate he, too, was tired and had set up in his mind a routine to stop himself from falling into a heavy slumber. It was only too easy at that height.

He woke Stubbles and gave him the watch. He woke Sorrel and they sat on the floor and talked as they had done soon after the emergency. He was fighting hard to stay totally awake.

They were sitting on the floor of the flight-deck when they heard a shrill whistle above the engine noise. Stubbles was sitting with two fingers in his mouth. His left hand was pointing to the orange-coloured radar screen. Martin moved quickly to the captain's seat.

"I was looking at the weather," said Stubbles. "Guess what?"

There was a small dot on the top right hand corner of the rectangular radarscope. Martin adjusted the nose-scanner until the dot appeared in the very centre of the screen. It moved quickly to the left and out of view. Then, mysteriously, it came in view and crossed the scanner lengthwise. It left the screen again.

"At that speed," said Martin, "it must be a fighter. At our height, about thirty miles. We are closing on it."

"Well, it could be a routine training exercise," said Stubbles in a voice which was giving away nothing. "We're a long way away from any enemies."

"Come on now, there's a squadron of MIGs in Mozambique," said Martin. "We're just about in range."

The dot, bigger now, re-emerged on the screen.

"My guess is that he's searching for something," said Martin. "Us, I reckon."

"Why?"

"I can think of several million bucks' worth just fifteen feet behind your arse."

"You're kidding."

"It's the final pattern in the jig-saw. Now, do we turn and try and hide in that bank of thunderheads over to port? Or do we brazen it out by just going straight ahead and taking no notice?"

"He's still in the search pattern," said Stubbles. "He should have us on his radar by now. Jesus, we should be bursting right out of it at this size."

The engineer was getting excited. His voice was staccato and even more shrill than normal.

"I could do with a fix," said Martin.

"By dead reckoning we are one hundred miles north west of the Comoro Islands, two hundred miles from the Mozambique coast."

"Nicely, friend Stubbles. First you fly the plane and now you're navigating. What next?"

"Try me on the horses."

"I wish I had," said Martin in an even tone. "Now just hold it, my old son, there she is again."

Now the dot on the radar had transferred itself to the tinted windscreen, glinting in the sun, ten miles away. It was flying across their path and turned steeply towards them. The two aircraft closed at a combined air speed of more than a thousand miles an hour.

Sorrel was awake. She turned to Martin and said, "What do you mean, jig-saw?"

Martin said, "You and the Mafia I can understand. There was something else I could never quite understand. I thought I'd got it when I saw the Russian spy plane. If that's a MIG then the jig-saw is absolute."

The MIG was steering directly for the Hercules' radome, banking steeply to the right at the very last moment. It began to circle, five hundred feet above them. It kept a steady pace with the Hercules.

"What does he want?"

"Listen out."

They heard the crackle of the static on the air-to-air frequency. Suddenly the 'transmit' button was depressed in the other aircraft. It was Umboto who was obviously reading from a prepared script. He read slowly with difficulty on the long words.

"Unidentified aircraft, this is Captain Umboto of the Mozambique Air Force. You are trespassing on the Mozambique air space. You are instructed to land. Proceed Mocímboa Airport, steering course two six zero. Acknowledge this message and proceed as directed. Do you read?"

The 'transmit' clicked off.

Martin pushed his transmitter button.

"Bullshit," he said succinctly. "We are two hundred miles from Mozambique."

"I repeat my instruction." Umboto was still obviously reading what he was saying. "You are to land immediately. Steer two six zero."

Martin chewed on his lip. He turned to Sorrel.

"Strap the co-pilot into the bunk. Then yourself. I smell something very very nasty coming up."

*　　*　　*

In the rear seat of the MIG, Uglov groaned once again and fought off a sudden new attack of nausea. He dare not take off his oxygen mask for more than a few seconds at that atmosphere and he closed his eyes and gripped hard on to the cockpit wall while he regained control of himself.

"What did he say?" he asked Umboto through the intercom.

"Bullshit."

"What is bullshit?"

"He will not land. What now?"

"Tell him that you will open fire if he does not change course immediately."

"Okay, boss."

*　　*　　*

The MIG had throttled back to a near stalling speed and lost height gradually until it was less than half a mile in front of the Hercules. Martin and Harry watched it apprehensively.

"Now what?" said Martin.

The MIG waggled its wings and turned sharply to the right.

"Follow me in this direction," said Umboto's voice.

"Get lost," said Martin. There was a terseness in his voice which made Stubbles look around at him.

"Do you think he means it, all that about firing?" he said.

"The French knew where we were going. I'm damn sure those bastards do too."

"But, hell's bells, we are miles away from their air space."

"All the better for them. VHF that no one can hear, no radar to track what's happening. They could bring us out of the sky just like that and who the hell would know about it?"

"The life history recorders would be recovered."

Stubbles was talking about the two flight recorders on board which kept a record of every conversation of the flight-deck on a thirty minute loop system.

"Hey," he said, almost chirpily. "Anyone who picks this up. We are Juliet Mike Oscar and we are under threat and duress by a MIG 21 fighter near Mozambique. Do you follow me? The other guy is threatening to shoot us down. Okay, now it's on record."

"A nice try, Stubbles," said Martin. "But you can bet your engineer's licence that there'll be a Russian destroyer down there somewhere to pick up any pieces."

Umboto came on sharply with total clarity. They could sense the fear and excitement in his voice.

"This is my final warning. Obey my instructions or I will open fire. I am entirely serious."

"Shit, he means it," said Martin. "Emergency procedure. Sorrel, tighten that mask on Harry's face and get one from the locker for yourself. Strap yourself in and brace yourself for anything. Stubbles, get on to oxygen pronto. Then into your own seat and wait for my signal. Then depressurise, got it?"

"Got it."

Martin almost ripped the oxygen mask from its box beneath his seat, plugged it in and slammed it on his face. He snapped the auto pilot to its 'off' position and looked around.

"Are we all on oxygen?" he asked.

"All crew on," said Stubbles.

"Depressurise."

"Emergency depressurisation on."

"Stand by for emergency evasive action."

Stubbles pulled the red lever and there was a sudden hissing. All of them felt sharp jabs of pain in their ears.

"May Day, May Day, Juliet Mike Oscar under threat of attack from Mozambique fighter aircraft, position thirty miles west of Comoro Islands."

Martin banked the Hercules hard to the left and pushed the wheel violently away from him.

Juliet Mike Oscar had just entered a steep descent when Uglov pushed the 'fire' button in the MIG.

*   *   *

It was the crisp delivery of the phrase 'get lost' that decided Yefgeni Uglov to bring the Hercules down at any cost.

He had hoped that the warning would be enough, that the American would turn meekly westwards and that he could bring them home and thus gain the kind of credit with his masters which would offset the scandal of the previous night.

But was he in a fit state to make such a decision? The cabin heater in the MIG was fiercely inaccurate and the heavy, rancid smell of the palm oil was everywhere, sickly and cloying, even in his oxygen mask. The oxygen had helped at first and had eased the total discomfort of the hangover enough for him to ensure that Umboto took off safely, although he, Uglov, had nearly fainted as the other pilot had used the rocket assisted take-off system for no other reason than to show off to his conquests of last night. The extra gravity had distorted his already weakened body. He felt as though his whole face was being spread like a *blini* against the headrest.

He had moaned and the giant African in front had howled with laughter and accelerated even more.

He hoped that his tampering with the fuse of the missile would be effective, that it would merely show the other pilot dramatically that he meant what he said.

Then came those two words. 'Get lost'.

Any further thoughts of morality froze in the Russian pilot's brain.

Very well, you warmongering jackal, he thought. The litany of Soviet propaganda came readily to his mind now. This arrogant bringer of death must be stopped. Uglov wrenched himself with a furious effort into the state of mind which he required to act decisively and see the operation through.

"My controls," he shouted to the black pilot in front of him.

Umboto's voice was sulky. "This is my target," he said.

Uglov slid forward the lever which overrode the trainee pilot's control column and rudder bars.

"My controls. You'll get the medal, Comrade Umboto, have no fear."

Uglov made a wide, banking turn and flew on a reciprocal course away from the Hercules for thirty seconds until he was ten miles away from his target. He circled several times while he opened a perspex-covered, red-lined box on the panel in front of him and selected a switch marked PREPARE MISSILE.

He waited for ten seconds until a bright blue light began to flash in the box and there was a reedy constant note in his earphones.

He glanced towards the Hercules which continued to fly confidently along its original course as though nothing had happened. Uglov brought the MIG gently on to the same course. He continued to hold the same near stalling speed.

"Now listen, Umboto. Very shortly I am going to increase speed to mach 1.5. I am going to release the missile, as near as I can estimate, at six kilometres from the target. The missile is set for detonation at about 1.5 kilometres from the target. As soon as the missile is released, I shall bank steeply to the right and climb. There is still a danger that we will be damaged by the blast."

"I understand."

"Be prepared to eject immediately. You know the drills. I have spent enough time teaching you."

"Okay, boss."

"Don't call me boss." Uglov's voice was testy.

"Sorry, boss."

Umboto was suddenly deflated, he realised. Maybe it was the thought of ejection from the supersonic fighter at that height. Or maybe it was a fear of the water below. He saw the pilot in front of him make the sign of the cross.

"No mumbo-jumbo, Umboto," he snapped. "Stand by."

Uglov eased forward the throttle and released the air brakes which had slowed the MIG down to its present speed. The fighter jolted forward with the increased engine power. Once again he felt his head jammed against the rest behind him. Then he applied full boost until the mach meter showed that they had passed through the sonic barrier. There was no other indication except for a faint vibration of the fuselage.

The Hercules was already outlined against the vivid blue sky, just slightly higher than them. The MIG engine bellowed power behind Uglov's back. His hangover was forgotten and now he was tense and exhilarated by the action. His heart thumped and he felt the whole of his body springing back to life.

The radar in combination with a small computer would normally have triggered the detonator in the missile's solid fuel propulsion engines at precisely the distance he required. But now Uglov had to make the fatal guess at one thousand five hundred miles an hour, doing the job of both electronic instruments with his own mind, with no yardstick to draw on except his own experience.

The Hercules loomed large in his sight now, its engine vapour distorting the air five hundred feet above them. Ten kilometres, he estimated, eight, seven, six — fire. He pushed the release button and saw the dense white smoke of the missile streak away from under them. At the same time he noticed that the Hercules had begun to turn steeply away.

Immediately he put the control column hard to the right and pulled it towards him. The 'G' suit he was wearing was not sufficiently adjusted to prevent a sudden inrush of blood from his head. He heard Umboto scream. He automatically eased the control column to a normal level flight position. He remained blacked out for several seconds.

Even at that distance, the blast of the missile two miles away from him caught the MIG and threw it crazily around the sky as though it were a paper dart in a tornado.

*　　　*　　　*

The blast-wave hit Juliet Mike Oscar as she was descending at an angle of thirty-five degrees. The tail unit took the main brunt of the series of shock waves which engulfed the giant aircraft, threatening for several seconds to rip her to pieces. Without warning she was in the centre of a vast area of disturbed air and, deprived of aerodynamic security, she bucked and weaved and was tossed violently around the sky, her engines yowling unevenly as a series of vacuums overtook them, rendering them worthless at a time when the captain needed them most to control the Hercules and to stop her from flipping disastrously on to her back.

They did not hear the explosion on the flight-deck. The first indication was a sudden punch in all their backs by a force which held them immobile in their seats. Martin felt the control column fly out of his hands and snap against the instrument console in front of him. He could not move. The gravity held him in steel bands. It took all his strength, together with an extra dimension of power, to get forward and try to steady the wheel which rocked crazily from side to side.

Juliet Mike Oscar was out of control in a dive of fifty degrees, being borne forward by a secondary area of blast at a speed at which no designer had ever conceived she could fly.

The force should have ripped off her wings; indeed at the very worst of the maelstrom they bent upwards and downwards again to the very maximum limit of stress.

These were sounds which could be heard on the flight-deck. A thousand tuneless discords echoed through the cargo hull as every joint, weld, rivet, screw, anchor point, pylon and every square inch of the alloy fabric was put to the ultimate test of strength and design. She groaned, that aircraft, as sailing ships of old had groaned in any tempest. For those few seconds she was a living creature, roaring at this monumental affront to her strength and grace.

And then she began to dive, back in solid air now, her four Hamilton propellers straining to take her almost vertically to the sea below.

It was a critical test for the captain, too. His instinct was to pull the control column back sharply, to force her into level flight. Experience overcame that instinct. He allowed her to go ahead long enough for the groaning to stop so that they could be further away from the menace in the sky nearby.

He eased back on the controls and felt the elevator respond. The Hercules pulled out gradually and he saw the air speed drop to the steady three hundred knots at which he had been flying. She flew well, perfectly indeed.

Except that she pulled heavily to her left.

Martin had to ram his foot hard down on the right rudder to correct this pull.

With his right hand he motioned Stubbles back into the co-pilot's seat.

"Take the strain," he said.

The engineer's size made it difficult for him to put his foot fully down on the rudder pedal. But when he did so it eased the considerable effort which Martin was making.

Something was wrong, radically wrong. There was no time to look around and check the others on the flight-deck.

"Your guess?" asked Martin.

"The tail stinger. They've blown off the tail stinger."

"That figures."

"She'll fly, but it's going to take a hell of a lot of sweat."

"Can you hold her in a circle?"

"I guess so, Captain."

"Try. I want to go back."

"Hey, Captain, I can't fly this bucket."

"I'm going back. She'll fly level now. Just let her ease her way round."

Martin watched Stubbles for a few moments. He could see the strain on the other man's face as he straightened his leg on the rudder bar and he could hear him breathing hard into the oxygen mask.

"Good boy," he said. "Stay like that."

He put his foot back on the pedal to help Stubbles and began to talk quickly and quietly.

"Now listen, all of you," he said. "This guy means what he says. He *will* shoot us down if we don't comply. Okay, so we can land over there. If we do that means you can bet your sweet arses that they'll try us as mercenaries. That means a firing squad. And I'm pretty damn sure that that's what the game has been all the way along the line.

"Now, a while back I broke open a Red-eye missile and launcher from a crate in the cargo hold. I reckon to take a chance with it through the cargo door.

"Now you men know that there's a fifty-fifty chance that the Red-eye is going to turn round and hit us right up our own Allisons. Right? So I'll take a vote. It's your lives. Be quick. Do we land her or take the gamble? Stubbles?"

"Can you do it?"

"I can try. Harry — if you are awake?"

Harry's voice sounded weak. But he said, "Go ahead. Hit the bastard."

"Sorrel, whatever you say, you're outvoted."

Stubbles butted in, tapping Martin on his knee. "The MIG. He's right beside us."

"Listen out."

It was Uglov who spoke. The Russian accent hit them immediately.

"Unidentified aircraft, you now see that we mean exactly

what we say. That explosion was intended to incapacitate you. It has clearly succeeded in doing that. Now proceed as directed or the result may be your total destruction."

Martin said, "We are repairing damage. Then we will follow your instructions, you bastard."

He turned to Stubbles.

"Okay, you take her."

Martin took a deep breath of oxygen and unplugged the mask, keeping it over his face.

*   *   *

Uglow recovered to find the MIG climbing frantically, its engine at full power. He wrenched the throttle back and the sudden loss of boost and the effect of gravity brought the aircraft to what seemed to be almost a standstill in mid-air. He flipped it on to its back and saw the Hercules diving towards the sea. He pulled the controls towards him and began to dive after it.

He was still not sure that he had not damaged it so badly that it would crash. But then, as he approached it from above, he saw it pull gradually from its steep descent and begin to level off. He approached it gingerly and watched it begin to circle. He made several passes and on the third of these he saw the small piece of tailplane streaming horizontally from the Hercules.

It was only then that he knew just exactly how successful his impromptu, pure guesswork missile attack had been.

*   *   *

Clutching the oxygen unit in his hand, Martin made his way rapidly across the flight-deck to the steps to the entry well. He paused there and plugged the oxygen lead into another point. As he charged his lungs once again, he looked up and saw Sorrel's pale face. She was watching him with eyes filled with concern over her own mask. He winked at her and disappeared through the cargo hatch.

Even at twenty thousand feet the newly depressurised cargo hold was bitterly cold and ice was forming on the roof and bulkheads. Martin had to slither across the crates, gasping loudly for breath between the red-coloured emergency oxygen points.

Finally he reached the rear of the massive hold where the Red-eye missile lay as he had left it, the four foot long cylinder already in its launching tube.

He plugged in the loadmaster's oxygen point.

"Stubbles, get ready to adjust the trim when I open the cargo door. She'll go tail heavy with the suction and try to rear up."

"Roger."

"Warning light coming on. Any sign of the enemy?"

"He's just ambling all around us, looking for damage, I guess."

Martin took a webbing strap attached to an anchor point on the port paratroop door and fixed a harness on to himself. He had about twelve feet of movement. But he knew that the suction once the huge rear cargo door had opened upwards would be enough to snatch him out of the aircraft, helpless as he dangled in its slip-stream. He released the safety catch over the button which operated the hydraulically upward lifting door and pushed, praying quietly that the explosion had not distorted the frame and so jammed the mechanism. The door slid upwards and immediately there was a fierce rushing noise as Martin faced a large expanse of freezing blue air. He picked up the Red-eye and took up his firing position.

"Where is he?" he asked.

"He's just slunk away to starboard. Maybe he's making another run at us. You should be seeing him."

"Has he said anything?"

"Nothing."

Martin lay on the lower cargo hatch and felt his hands become almost numb with the sudden coldness.

"I've got him. Get ready."

The MIG had appeared from Martin's left and now it turned and began to move in towards the Hercules tail plane. It was immediately behind the aircraft maybe five miles in distance but closing quickly.

Martin pulled the Red-eye hard into his shoulder and squeezed the pistol grip. There was a tingling vibration in the grip which meant that the missile was activated and ready.

He peered through the optical sight which lay in the blast guard which would protect his face from the missile's explosive propulsion and lined the MIG up in the very centre of the cross wires in the sights.

The Red eye is a simple ground-to-air missile designed for use by forward troops against low-flying aircraft. It has no sophisticated computers, just a straightforward infra-red heat-seeking guidance system.

He watched the fighter get bigger in his sights. He had no idea of the range of the missile and this was his biggest fear. He needed to hit the MIG or the Red-eye really would start to range about the sky looking for the heat of an engine nacelle. The MIG had one; but the Hercules had four.

He waited until he guessed the fighter was two miles away and still closing. He breathed in deeply to steady his aim and pushed the firing button with his thumb.

*   *   *

Uglov was elated as he whipped the MIG over and under the crippled transporter. All the guilt feelings of last night and the dreadful hangover had disappeared. His mission had been successful. The American was cringing on the radio.

In the front seat, Umboto was whooping and crowing with delight.

"Hey boss, they'll give us medals," he shouted. "We'll

have a great party tonight, eh? I'll get you four girls — how about that?"

Uglov made one more rapid pass under the Hercules and gave himself the pleasure of a long, slow, graceful roll before he turned suddenly to take one last look at his prey before heading for the coast and refuelling. He approached Juliet from the stern. He handed the controls to Umboto and took a Zenit 80 camera from a recess in the cockpit. Even if the American did not make an airport he, at least, would have the evidence to show that he had tried. He set the shutter speed and aperture and peered through the viewfinder at the other aircraft.

"Go as near to his tail as you can," he ordered Umboto.

The two or three seconds that it took Uglov to adjust the lens and bring the Hercules into prime focus probably cost their lives.

He saw the open cargo hatch at the rear of the big plane. Then for a split second he saw Martin Gore and the missile launcher.

In the very next second he saw the smoke of the Red-eye.

Umboto was already beginning to bank steeply away to his right when the missile hit the MIG squarely on its underbelly.

*　　　*　　　*

Throughout the morning there had been frantic activity at every Soviet Embassy and Legation throughout the length and breadth of the African continent. Telephone lines were in constant use to a myriad of Patriotic Front organisations and left-wing Trade Union groups as well as student leaders and others with direct access to anyone who would be prepared to flow on to the streets in protest. Messages were relayed by circuitous routes to activists and guerrillas, messages which contained much more sinister overtones.

The KGB had scented blood and now it was in full cry.

Newspapers in every emergent state were warned that a major announcement could be expected some time that afternoon.

In some cities excited youngsters, already skilled in the art of riot, began to make piles of stones in tactical points near to western embassies and installations. And the embassies, in turn, strengthened their guards and cancelled their traditional afternoon bridge sessions and sent their own agents scurrying into the downtown quarters to find out what the big reason was for today's affair.

It was a relatively regular game played by embassies all over the world. There were no written rules.

Students were the star players because they were young and excitable and quick to comprehend alleged injustices, and because they would willingly risk their lives in a stream of police bullets for the futile support of an unknown martyr in a far away land or a cause which just happened to sound revolutionary.

The Russians were the masters of the demonstration game. The KGB dictionary was packed with emotive names and issues which either whispered or yelled through a loud-hailer could be certain of fermenting every kind of protest from a one hour strike to a violent lethal demonstration, in which men, women and children were sacrificed in the name of protest.

There were few more emotive issues in black Africa at that time than that of arms for the white Rhodesians.

The preparations were elaborate.

A few minutes after the MIG trainer had taken off from Mocímboa Airport, a small chartered twin piston engined plane landed on the same runway carrying a four man team from the Tass newsagency bureau in Dar es Salaam.

The correspondent's task was two-fold. Firstly, he had to confirm urgently that the American aircraft had landed, and secondly, he had to interview the crew and secure an immediate admission that they were guilty. The second man would film and record it all for television.

The accompanying photographer was instructed to make

the kind of pictures which would prove the guilt beyond any doubt. The fourth man, a wire-photo operator, was to ensure that the still pictures were flashed to the nearest satellite injection station within minutes of being processed. Moscow would do the rest.

The release of the story was to be the signal for the distribution of millions of prepared leaflets which had been roneoed that morning, in every African language and dialect.

Protest meetings were already being called even though the organisers had not the slightest idea at that moment what it was that they were going to protest about.

As it had been in Djibouti so it was now through the whole of Africa. A continent was tingling with anticipation.

*   *   *

In Mocímboa the Tass team waited in the steaming midday heat. In the control tower they heard the exchanges between the MIG and the Hercules. They heard Martin tell Uglov that he was prepared to land. The correspondent was tempted at that point to flash a triumphant signal to Moscow, but a shrewdly developed second sense stopped him in time.

They waited with camera gear set up and the only photography shop in town fully prepared for the action to come. The wire-photo operator had established a contact with Dar es Salaam. They waited until they were sure that the MIG must have run out of fuel and then waited for another full hour until the correspondent made his disconsolate way to the local post office and filed the news.

After a further hour's wait, a Soviet destroyer off the Mozambique coast signalled that she had found wreckage from the MIG and the body of Major Yefgeni Uglov. There was no trace of any other aircraft.

In Moscow, Colonel-General Yuri Litvinoff read the cable and merely shrugged his shoulders. He ordered a one word signal to be sent to each of his senior operatives in Africa.

It was a matter of two or three hours before the tension dissipated throughout Africa.

The Russians are masters at fermenting protest. They are equal masters in the art of concealing their own mistakes, cloaking them in a haze of political inscrutability.

*   *   *

Shortly before noon, London time, as the two aircraft were coming together nine thousand miles away off the African coast, Natalia Rogov hurried along a seemingly endless passageway at Heathrow Airport from her Aeroflot flight. She ignored the welcoming posters, her eyes set on the signs marked 'transit passengers'. She wore a bright blue roll-necked sweater and faded jeans and the British Airport girl who checked her passport and ticket to New York found it difficult to reconcile this totally casual woman with the word DIPLOMAT stamped on her passport.

Her rank warranted minor VIP treatment but she waved the offer aside and hurried into the departure lounge. She had to queue restlessly to change her Norodni Bank travellers cheques and glanced constantly at the departures board.

She made her way through the crowded lounge to a bank of circular white telephone booths. All of them were in use and she hovered almost threateningly over a salesman from Miami who was yelling a final farewell to his sister in Bradford.

It may have been the fierceness of her stare or the firmness of her breasts, but he stopped talking quickly and made way for the Russian woman.

From her handbag she took a small address book and dialled the Soviet Embassy and asked for extension two six.

"Rogov," she said.

"Ah yes," said a man's voice. "I have a message for you. Uncle says that the party is definitely on. Ask Peter for details when you arrive."

148

"Thank you," she said and slammed the receiver on its hook.

She looked at the departure board and saw that TWA flight 128 to New York was on final call at gate 18. She almost ran along the equally long airport finger and was the last passenger to board the 747.

One hour later, as the lifeless, mangled body of Yefgeni Uglov lay face upwards in the Indian Ocean, she ordered a Jack Daniels bourbon on the rocks and tried hard to concentrate on a weighty book on the Anthropology of the African Tribes.

After a while she gave up and gratefully accepted a near pornographic paperback from her neighbour but soon found that equally difficult to read.

She closed her eyes, but she could not sleep. So many things were happening. She felt desperately trapped in that giant tube 30,000 feet over the Atlantic.

*   *   *

"Pan, pan, pan. Durban radio. This is Juliet Mike Oscar, Hercules transport. We are ten miles to the north east of you. We have a badly damaged tail unit and extremely low fuel reserve. Request permission for immediate landing. We are at flight level one hundred, heading two one zero magnetic. Over."

"Pan. Juliet Mike Oscar, Durban radio. You are clear to land at Pietermaritzburg, a military airfield. Steer two eight zero magnetic. Change to one two five decimal five. Over and out."

"Pan. Durban radio, Juliet Mike Oscar. Negative Pietermaritzburg. Our fuel level is critical. We are seven miles from you and beginning descent. Request priority landing. Over."

"Pan. Juliet Mike Oscar, Durban radio. Wait."

All three men and Sorrel had taken their turns at the

controls, Martin steering and the others bracing their strength against the powerful force of the rudder.

The captain and co-pilot had held lengthy debates about the possibility of making a low run directly into Rhodesia over the narrowest part of Mozambique. It would have meant less than two hundred miles of hostile territory and would have ensured their arrival in Salisbury. But after long consideration they had opted against. Flying was difficult enough in these conditions. Low flying would have been near-suicidal and they had no idea what other opposition they might expect.

Harry had insisted on leaving the bunk and taking his right-hand seat although he was clearly often on the point of collapse. He refused to listen to Martin's arguments.

They were all of them shaken by the suddenness and the viciousness of the attack. And the atmosphere on the flight-deck had been subdued and apprehensive with frequent glances all around the aircraft and with the radar in constant use.

A strong following wind had helped to speed them over the Mozambique channel. This had cheered Stubbles, who spent much of the rest of that flight working out detailed fuel calculations and shaking his head with pessimism.

It was not until they had established that the flat green stretch beneath them was the South African coast that Sorrel opened a bottle of Scotch and handed half filled cups to each of the men.

They could only assume, even now, that they would be given landing permission in South Africa. They had decided not to make any approach over the airwaves until there was no question of their being refused. Even so this response from Durban was disturbing.

"Why a military airfield?" asked Martin.

"Because we are a military aircraft," said Harry.

"How do they know?"

"It's you that's paranoid. I don't think we're the first Hercules to pass this way bearing arms for Ian Smith."

"Well, come what may, I'm going into Durban. If they don't clear us I'm going to set this bitch down on one of those beautiful beaches down there."

"Pan. Juliet Mike Oscar, Durban radio. You are clear to land as requested. We have you on radar. Maintain your present heading and rate of descent. You are priority one for landing. All other aircraft on this frequency change to one two six decimal five."

"Thank the good Lord for giving that guy a brain," said Martin. "Pre-landing checks, gentlemen, if you please."

*   *   *

There was an atmosphere approaching near euphoria on the flight-deck as they taxied off the runway and into a parking position at Durban. The landing itself had been difficult. At any other time it would have been treated as a full blown emergency. The physical effort by both pilots was enormous, as they strained against the weight of the rudder bar and landed on aileron and propeller pitch. Juliet yawed capriciously on the final landing roll and seemed willing at one time to leave the runway altogether and carve a track through the grass in the centre of the field.

Four fire engines and two ambulances had been waiting and they could see them from the flight-deck trailing away slowly, almost regretfully.

"Like dogs who had the bone taken away," said Martin grimly. "If they knew what was in the back of this ageing crate, I don't think they would have come quite so close."

The controller, a friendly voice, parked them several hundred yards from the handful of scheduled aircraft at the terminal. The ground director crossed his orange batons and they shut down the four engines.

Stubbles spoke in a Jimmy Durante voice.

"That was a somewhat superfluous gesture," he said. "Two

more minutes and they would have shut themselves down. We were that short on gas."

"Shutdown checks," said Martin. "Nose wheel and parking brake."

"Centred and set."

"Shutdown and NTS check all engines."

"Complete."

They ran through the checks at their usual brisk pace. It was not until the ground director confirmed by hand signal that the wheels had been chocked that Martin turned and saw that a mass of blood was welling through the bandages on Harry's right hand.

"Holy Cow," he said. "Since when?"

Harry was close to fainting again. His voice was weak and tired and lifeless.

"I've only just noticed. I must have been gripping the wheel like a trainee pilot."

"Okay, don't worry. Let's get you into one of those ambulances."

"I'll be okay."

Sorrel had opened the crew door and they heard a new voice.

"Good afternoon, gentlemen," said its owner, a punchy man with a huge belly wearing a white drill shirt and black trousers. "Department of Health. What was your point of embarkation, please?"

"Djibouti."

"Djibouti, eh. Where's that? Don't remember anyone ever coming from Djibouti."

He opened a small black book and ran through a list of cities.

"Can't see it anywhere," he said. "I'd better fumigate you anyway."

The man held up an aerosol spray and squirted it three times around the flight-deck. He repeated the operation in the cargo hold.

"A formality," he said. "Now then, any fresh fruit, meat, eggs or live animals on board?"

"No."

"May I see your cargo manifest?"

"We are carrying explosives."

"But no fresh fruit, meat, eggs or live animals?"

"No."

The man looked briefly at the aircraft's documents and handed them to Sorrel.

"There you are, young lady, and welcome to Durban." He looked at the two pilots.

"Man, what have you done to that hand?" he said.

* * *

He was a tall and lean man who spoke in a heavy, almost indecipherable Afrikaans accent. He introduced himself to Martin as Inspector Eisenberg of the Bureau of State Security. He took Martin from the aircraft into the airport building. They ignored customs and immigration and Eisenberg steered Martin to the small airport bar.

They ordered beer. Martin could see the Hercules at the end of the airport parking lot. A tall gantry had been built around the tailplane. Stubbles and two other engineers were making a close inspection of the damaged tailplane.

"I have to tell you, Captain Gore, that you couldn't have chosen a less fortunate time to land in this country, do you realise that?"

"I thought you were sympathetic to Rhodesia."

Eisenberg looked at him intently. "I am, of course I am. We all are. But if Smith cares to put himself on a limb there's no reason why we should have to go out and join him. Don't you realise that Cyrus Vance and our Prime Minister are sitting round the same table at this very moment in Pretoria? And Ian Smith himself is meeting with Vance later on today."

Martin downed his beer. He put the empty glass on to the counter and beckoned to the barman.

"Two more, please," he said.

"You haven't any money," the other man said. "I'll buy. We're a hospitable nation, Captain Gore. I hate to have to kick you out."

"Kick us out?"

"Come now, Captain, you are an intelligent man. We knew about you from the moment that you left Djibouti."

"How?"

"Because the Reds had set you up perfectly. You name would have been front page news all over Africa if that MIG had brought you down. There's very little that happens on this continent that my agency doesn't know about, Captain. The trouble is that it works in reverse, the other side keeps a pretty close watch on us. And that's a very big aeroplane out there to hide."

Martin perched himself on a bar stool and gazed gloomily at his reflection behind the bottles. His face was pale; there was an added gauntness to it. He felt that he had aged a few more years since leaving Karachi. He sipped at the second beer.

"So?" he questioned.

"So, Captain, I'm afraid that you and your crew are confined to this airport. We want you here for the shortest possible time. You will be given technical assistance for the damaged rudder tab in exchange for your telling our air force people about the way you brought down the MIG. Your co-pilot will have his hand attended to. But in the meantime you will speak to no one without my permission. As soon as your aircraft has been repaired and refuelled you will be escorted to your aircraft and you will take-off."

"I suppose that's reasonable in the circumstances," declared Martin. "But tell me one thing. I thought that most arms for Rhodesia came from this country."

"You're right," said Eisenberg. "At any other time you'd be given a much warmer welcome. But right at the moment you are, I'm afraid to say, nothing more than an embarrassment. A dangerous embarrassment, considering the talks that are going on in our capital."

There was a 'ping' on the Tannoy system followed by a short announcement in Afrikaans.

"Excuse me, Captain. That was for me."

Martin drank more beer and walked to the window where he could see the activity increasing around Juliet Mike Oscar. There were more engineers on the gantry now. The slender rudder stinger was being lowered to the ground. From where he stood Martin could see little sign of damage. Stubbles, perched on tiptoe at the very top of the structure, was peering into the inside of the tail.

The agent returned to the bar. He sat on the stool next to Martin and waited for the barman to get out of earshot.

"The old joke about good news and bad news," he said. "They estimate that it will take six hours only to repair your aircraft. That's good news. You should be away soon after lunch."

"Whose estimate?"

"Your own engineer. The bad news is that I have orders from Pretoria which have come from the Prime Minister personally. I have to tell you, Captain, that if there is one single press inquiry about your mission involving the Republic of South Africa I must arrest you and your crew and impound the aircraft. It is the only way of avoiding embarrassment. My government cannot afford to face a charge of hypocrisy."

Martin spun round on his stool. The agent recoiled as though the aviator was going to strike him. Instead he was surprised to see the other man grinning broadly.

"Do you know something, I haven't felt quite so unwanted since I flew six crates of live rattlesnakes from Mexico to Chicago. Everyone was being really nice, but weren't they all in a hurry to see me on my way!"

"I don't suppose that we could do much more than fine you and confiscate your load," said Eisenberg. "We know the owner of the aircraft, Mr Ragnelli. We've done business with him before. He'll pay."

"I wonder," said Martin.

Eisenberg stood up. "Please wait here, Captain Gore, until the girl returns with your co-pilot," he said. "I'll do all I can. I trust you to use your common sense and not talk to anybody. It's in your own interest."

The agent began to walk away then he stopped. He turned and came back to Martin and took several rand notes from his wallet. "I know the rules about drinking and flying, Captain," he said. "But you've had quite a journey. Have some coffee on me."

*　　　*　　　*

Natalia pressed her customs clearance form into the hands of a fat guard at the gate of the TWA terminal and went immediately to the news stand in the departures area. It was 2.30 pm in New York and the first edition of the *Post* had just arrived at John F Kennedy Airport.

The page one headline told of a family slaying on the west side. She threw the paper angrily into a waste can.

Five minutes later Natalia was in an embassy car driven at speed in a honking, roaring stream of traffic towards Manhattan.

As the car emerged from the Queens Mid-town tunnel and turned into Third Avenue she ordered the driver to stop. She went to another news stand and bought a later edition of the same paper.

Back in the car she scanned each news page thoroughly before slamming the paper on the floor as the car drew into the United Nations complex.

*　　　*　　　*

Eisenberg drove them to the waiting Hercules. Even as they approached her they could see that the gantry was being taken to pieces and they watched the massive rudder unit sway from side to side as Stubbles tested it from the flight-deck. Four fire engines flanked the aircraft, their blue lights flashing and their crews clearly at immediate readiness.

"A trifle melodramatic," said Martin casually to Eisenberg.

The South African did not reply. His friendly manner had disappeared. He was clearly tense and angry. He braked the car with unnecessary ferocity under the port wing and switched off the engine.

"Before you get into that plane, all of you, I have three things to tell you," he said in a voice which was ice-like. He intended every word to be heard.

"The first of these concerns a gross abuse of the hospitality which my Government has shown to you. Miss Francis was unwise enough to slip her escort and to make a telephone call to New York from the Royal Hotel in Durban. I do not know the substance of that telephone call, but I do know that she has rendered you all liable to imprisonment. Her behaviour has stretched my tolerance to its limit."

Harry rounded on the girl. He was livid and he raised his freshly bandaged hand against her face.

"Stupid whore," he shouted. "Who were you calling?"

"My brother," she said primly. "I wanted my family to know I was safe."

"Secondly," said Eisenberg ignoring them. "I should tell you that your very presence in the Republic has put my government in a most embarrassing position. I am instructed directly by the Cabinet to tell you that from the moment you leave this airport, you do not exist."

The tall South African drummed his fingers on the steering wheel and looked directly ahead.

"You will not use your radio at any time. You will fly a direct course from Durban to Salisbury. Air traffic control zones have been notified that you will be passing through their territory and other aircraft will be steered clear of you. You will be escorted by two fighters of the South African Air Force."

Eisenberg turned and looked directly into Martin's eyes.

"If you divert from your course or use your radio for anything but the direst emergency, they have orders to shoot you down."

It was Martin's turn to be frigid now. "You can't be serious," he said. "This is a civilised country."

"We aim to stay that way, Captain Gore. I am anxious that the world should remain completely unaware of any South African involvement in your mission. As you are aware, there has been serious rioting in some of our townships. We can do without pressure from the outside."

"What happens if we are forced to divert from our course by bad weather?" asked Martin.

"Don't divert," said Eisenberg. "Don't breathe a word into your radios."

"And if we throw?"

"Don't come back." He pulled a sheaf of paper from the inside of his jacket.

"This is a telex message received an hour ago from the French authorities in Djibouti. All African-police forces will have been circulated with a description of you and your crew. You are wanted on a murder charge."

*   *   *

There was little talk on that flight-deck during the last leg which took them high over Swaziland, the soft hills of the Transvaal stretching interminably away to their left. Harry had started to yell at Sorrel but Martin had silenced him. They had needed every ounce of energy for the Durban take-off. They were tired and the pain from Harry's hand made concentration doubly difficult for him.

Stubbles had logged six hours' sleep out of the past thirty-six and was curled in the bunk within minutes of completing the post take-off engineering checks.

Sorrel sat friendless and worked nonchalantly at a cross-word in that morning's Durban newspaper.

Martin and Harry were equally tired. They were pleased to be able to take the Hercules to cruising height and leave the work to the autopilot, and even more pleased that there was no need, for the first two hours at least, for them to chat to men on the ground.

They saw little of the two South African Hunters which sat ten thousand feet above them, but they could hear the two pilots talking with gruff good humour about football, food and women. They heard two other fighters move in to relieve the original escort, but the two new men were not loquacious.

They finally came into sight with a series of spectacular line-abreast loops and rolls from which they eventually broke and fought a mock dogfight immediately ahead of the lumbering transporter.

"Clever bastards," said Harry, with grudging admiration.

The fighters peeled away and Juliet Mike Oscar crossed the Limpopo River and entered Rhodesian air space.

"Did you see the weapons they were carrying?" said Martin. "They really meant it."

"I had no doubt of that from the very beginning," said Harry. He was having difficulty holding the slide rule in his right hand while he adjusted it with his left. He held it up to the perspex screen.

"One hour and seven minutes to touchdown," he said. "Shall I tell them we're coming?"

"You're sure we're in Rhodesian air space?" said Martin.

"Five minutes in."

"All right, tell them we're coming up the drive."

It was then that Martin saw the revolver, held in a slim, carefully manicured hand, touch the back of Harry's neck and rest immediately below the hair line.

"You'll say nothing to anybody."

Sorrel's voice was completely composed through their earphones. Martin turned and saw her in the engineer's seat. There was a half smile on her face and her chin was thrust slightly forward, emphasising the determination.

"Listen very carefully," she said. They sensed that she

had been rehearsing this moment for the past two hours. "In the first place, we are not going to Salisbury or any other airport in Rhodesia. My instructions are to deliver this load to an airstrip on the Angolan border and that's exactly where you are going to take me."

"Now wait a minute . . ." Martin's brain, already shredded by fatigue, was reeling.

"Shut up," she said. "Just in case you have any thoughts of doing anything heroic, I'm telling you that this is a US police short-stop revolver that fires a simple revolving missile. It'll blow most of his head off, but it won't damage the fabric of the aircraft.

"We're not landing in Rhodesia because Mr Ragnelli doesn't want us to land in Rhodesia."

"You talked to him?"

"Of course I did. If this consignment gets to Rhodesia, Captain Gore, apart from the fact that there'll be no money anyway, all four of us will spend the rest of our lives looking over our shoulders for Ragnelli's hit men."

"So what's the deal?"

"There's no deal. We leave the arms with a Ragnelli customer in Angola. They'll refuel you and you deliver the aircraft to Zaire. In Kinshasa there will be economy class tickets which will take us back to Brussels."

"Why no cash in Rhodesia?"

"Because I'm the only one who knows the code which will get it out of the bank. And I'm not risking my neck for a few lousy bucks."

Martin was looking at the revolver. It was squat and the barrel was fat and short. He turned to the girl. She was relaxed. She smiled at him.

"It's a hair trigger," she said. "I've fired it over a hundred times in demonstrations for Murphy. So don't risk Harry's head."

From the corner of his eye, Martin saw that Stubbles was fast asleep in the bunk.

"You won't get any help from the little guy," said the girl softly. "He's crashed. Not a hope."

"Bitch," said Martin. He had nothing else to say.

"Of course I'm a bitch," she spat. "A surviving bitch. Steer two eight zero and stay close to the Botswana border."

"You've worked that out?"

"It isn't that difficult. Your immediate destination is the Victoria Falls. Then you fly along the Caprivi Strip until you pick up a beacon on one one three megahertz. It will be tramitting the letter 'R' at thirty second intervals. You identify yourself by flashing your landing lights in the letter 'G'."

"All that in one telephone call from Ragnelli?"

"We've been operating the procedure for months. They are regular customers."

"Who?"

"UNITA. They fought the Cubans in Angola."

Martin sighed heavily.

"Okay," he said with supreme reluctance. "Take the gun away from Harry's head and I'll turn left. Slowly she brought her hand down and sat, almost primly, the revolver on her lap.

Harry had not uttered a sound since he had felt the pressure on his neck. He stared ahead and shook himself slightly.

"Two eight zero," he said and switched the auto pilot off. "They watched the compass spin slowly to the required course.

"And what about our hosts on the ground?" said Martin. They're watching us, you know, every move we make."

"You'll just have to keep out of their way," snapped the girl. "You were prepared to take the chance over Mozambique."

"The Rhodesians have a sophisticated air defence system," Martin said in a matter-of-fact tone. "They will have plotted us on radar long before we entered their air space, they will have watched that turn and, right at this moment, they'll be smelling a double-cross."

"So?"

"So, dear girl, they are surrounded by hostile forces and if they think for a moment that these weapons are going to the guerrillas, they won't hesitate to blow us out of the sky."

"Then you had better get down good and low. That's what you're good at."

It was then that Martin's temper snapped.

"You haven't the slightest bloody idea, have you?" he shouted suddenly. "This poor, ancient airframe has been submitted to stresses which would have automatically grounded it for months in any air force. It was dangerous when we set out, it's been bent by missiles, strained in that landing at Djibouti and the rudder is held together with piano wire and string. If I have to make any sharp manoeuvres at low level, I could kill all of us . . ."

Martin was interrupted by a stern and unyielding voice from the ground.

"Unidentified aircraft on two eight zero resume your original course and contact Bulawayo Radio immediately."

"Who was that?" asked Harry.

"I would guess it was our reception committee. We'll go down, make a normal descent and fly up the border."

They were losing height steadily when they heard the same deep and ominous voice again. It said simply, "Unidentified Aircraft, you are trespassing in Rhodesian air space. Unless you resume your original course and height immediately, you make yourself liable to retaliatory action."

Five minutes later, as they continued to descend, as the altimeter read ten thousand feet, Martin saw a number of flashes in the deepening evening gloom ahead and to the left of them and then saw small white puff-balls grow in the sky.

"Flak," he said simply. "Somebody wake Stubbles."

"I'm awake," said the engineer. He was half way across the flight-deck, trying to adjust his eyes in the difficult light. "Excuse me, miss, I'd better take over."

Stubbles did not see the gun until Sorrel stood up and eased her way out of his seat. She beckoned him to sit down. He blinked at her.

"No one can say this flight is not lacking in bewilderment," he said.

Martin had turned the aircraft steeply to the right. But

almost immediately, there was another cluster of puff-balls straight ahead of them.

"Hold on!" he shouted and put the Hercules into a steep side-slip to the left. Stubbles had just completed fastening his harness at that moment. The three men were secure in their seats.

Sorrel Francis could not hold on. She rose vertically and then flashed horizontally across the spacious flight-deck and crashed her head against the sharp corner of a storage box. Her skull was crushed instantly. As the three men fought to control the fast plummeting aircraft, she lay dead on the plastic-covered floor. There was a surprised expression on her face.

*　　　*　　　*

Darkness hid them as they flew low over the Botswana border. Martin relied heavily on the forward radar to keep them safely over the undulating countryside below. He was not expecting any further fire from the ground, but he could not be sure for a moment that Rhodesian fighters were not scanning the sky for them.

The navigation light switches remained at 'off'. The cabin interior lighting was left to the very minimum. Martin had only time for a momentary glimpse in the eerie glow behind him to see Harry and Stubbles lifting the girl's body and placing it in the bunk. Stubbles covered her with a sleeping bag. Harry swabbed the blood from the floor.

No one said a word. They flew steadily south-west until they were a hundred miles into Botswana. Martin brought Juliet slowly up through a thin layer of cirrus and they were suddenly flying into a black night in which every star and planet twinkled and glowed so vividly that they felt as though they were flying among them.

He handed over to Harry and went back to the bunk. He

pulled back the cover and looked at Sorrel's face. Stubbles had closed her eyes. The surprised expression had gone. But for the blood which had matted on the side of her head, she might have been sleeping peacefully.

Martin touched her cheek with his hand. Even as he did so he realised ruefully that only a few minutes ago he himself would willingly have stoved her head in.

"Poor bloody kid," he said. "You just wanted to be the chief rat in the sewer."

He covered her face and went back to his seat.

"It's sort of time for a board meeting, don't you think?" he said. "Let us consider our position. We are smack bang at three thousand feet over Africa. At least three countries are prepared to shoot us down. The others will probably put us in front of firing squads. Any thoughts?"

"We've got two hours' fuel," said Stubbles. "Which is not exactly going to get us to Atlantic City."

The captain pondered this for a few moments.

"Well then, let's do some business," he said quietly. "They all want to fight each other down there. It's a seller's market and we're the sellers."

"What have you got in mind?" said Harry.

"Once upon a time," said Martin, "during a period of unemployment I made a few bob by cautioning off horses at the Marlborough Horse Fair. They reckoned that I should have taken it up full time. Pity I didn't."

"So what?" said Harry.

"So I want you to give me a frequency that the whole of Africa can listen to."

"You're joking."

"I'm being bloody, deadly serious, Harry Black. Let me speak to the people."

Harry selected the most universal frequency he could find.

"You're on the air, Captain and cue you."

Martin took a deep breath.

He pushed the 'transmit' button and assumed a powerful voice as though he were talking to a group of farmers around a ring.

"Ladies and gentlemen," he said. "I'd like to welcome you all to the great flying arms auction of the air."

"You're crazy," said Harry.

"My assistant here says I'm crazy, ladies and gentlemen. Take it from me that I am crazy. I must be crazy to sell at prices like this. Everything is going at rock bottom prices.

"We're selling the kind of merchandise that only we can sell and at prices that even the thinnest of your wallets can afford. Take it from me, good people, you could scour the gun markets of the world for bargains like this and you'll never see the like again. Welcome to Captain Gore's flying emporium. We're in business."

"Fool," said Harry. But even he was laughing.

"Of course I'm a fool," shouted Martin. "My assistant says I'm a fool. I am a fool. This merchandise is not only new, its unused, untouched by human hand.

"Gather round and I'll show you. I'm not just here today and gone tomorrow. I'm here today and gone today."

Martin was calm, but his eyes flashed with delight as he looked out into the night. He waggled Juliet's wings with the release of his tension.

"Sorry that there are no catalogues. You know what printers are like. But let me describe lot one.

"We have five hundred anti-personnel mines, activated, would you believe, by the heat of your very bodies. Bury them in the ground, ladies and gentlemen, brothers and sisters, and watch them grow. Step within six yards of them and they'll flower in front of your very eyes. Or leap into the air and they'll explode into a gorgeous profusion of gold colour and then they'll cut you in half. Mind you, if you happen to be a child collecting butterflies maybe, they'll do even more. They'll cut your head right off. Now do I have a bid, ladies and gentlemen? We guarantee immediate delivery but the terms, and here's the only condition, are strictly cash."

Martin laughed aloud and looked at the stars for applause.

"Now while you're making up your minds on that, how about a real temptation? How about one hundred and fifty Red-eye missiles which come to you complete with launcher all packed in a hand-made pinewood case complete with a book of instructions?

"It's guaranteed to bring down helicopters, fighters, bombers, you name the flying bird and it'll kill. I tell you a baby could use this one straight from its case. I'll personally vouch for that. It's what you've all been looking for."

Martin paused and listened. He heard Stubbles say, "Hey don't stop — keep it up. Great."

"Very well," said Martin. "Now ladies and gentlemen, you've kept your hands in your pockets for far too long. You're in danger of losing out on one of the great cut-price shopping sprees of our time. Now let's hear some bids. I'll join both lots together. What do I hear? Do I hear fifty thousand dollars? You can't go wrong. Every item comes with a money back guarantee if it doesn't kill or maim the other chap. And just one other thing, these mines and missiles and every weapon in my treasure trove are absolutely impartial. They'll kill rats and blacks and Chinamen, every damn colour down there on that planet. They'll kill women and children and animals with absolute and complete disregard for race or colour. Have no fear, good people, these are the real McCoy."

Martin paused. Sweat was streaming down his face. There was silence on the radio but he was hot now. Nothing was going to stop him.

"Now you may wonder how we came to have these hard-to-get commodities. I have to tell you without breaking a confidence that they were the property of a gentleman down on his luck, namely the State of Rhodesia. He couldn't afford them, maybe you can. I'm sure you can indeed at these prices.

"Perhaps I can interest you in some M 16 rifles as well. We've got a nice lot of those in the toy department. You have again my personal undertaking that this rifle is so effective that it will make a hole the size of a penny in your front and leave a hole in your back not six inches wide, not eight inches wide, not ten inches wide. I guarantee a hole a foot wide. And if that's not good enough for you, I'll guarantee that it'll take off an arm or leg at the thigh and most of your bottom

166

with one shot. Now then come on, let's see a few hands, good people, because we haven't got that amount of time."

They were circling now over the Mahabe Depression. They listened out for some time. There was no response.

"Now are you sure I can't interest you in a thousand anti-tank projectiles? Or mortars or infra-red night sights that'll pick out and clearly identify the foreskin of a moth at a thousand paces?

"Here you are, ladies and gentlemen, and now I really will wait for the highest bidder. We're going to sit on this frequency, just waiting. But don't be shy there, sir. Step right up and name your price. Just as long as you can start bidding in United States dollars. On the other hand we don't mind pounds, francs, yen or escudos or rands or dinars or szloty. Do I hear five hundred thousand dollars? I don't hear five hundred thousand dollars. Or what do I hear? And incidentally the price will include three first class round the world tickets on an airline of our choice."

For the next thirty minutes there was constant chatter on the radio but it came entirely from other airmen near at hand.

A South African Airways 747 asked them what they were high on. A Central African Airways DC9 asked whether they'd send them a catalogue.

This was normal air-to-air banter but they managed to impress on the other pilots that they were deadly serious. Some of the others even suggested possible markets for the arms and the banter turned into a discussion.

Then they all became silent as a new voice from the ground joined them.

"This is Zambia radio. Stand by for a message."

"Do I hear a bid?" said Martin.

"Zambia radio. The message reads, You are welcome to land at Luzaka to discuss the sale of your cargo after inspection."

"I *did* hear a bid," said Martin. "Clearly a gentleman of discernment. And I should tell you something else, Mr Zambia, that you also have a Charlie one three zero aeroplane thrown in. You'll have to negotiate that with the owners but take it from me that it's going cheap. It needs a little overhaul here and there and it's got a few miles on the clock but it's a great bargain."

They wheeled again.

"Now can I interest anyone else in this load?"

Again there was silence and then a new voice joined them.

"This is Malawi. I am instructed to tell you that my government is also interested."

"So there we are, ladies and gentlemen, now I have two bidders. That gentleman sounded like he meant business," said Martin.

"Now, are there any more interested parties? Otherwise let's make this a straight bidding match between the two gentlemen."

There was a third voice. It was more distant than the others and less distinct.

"This is Entebbe control, Uganda. I have a message. Field Marshal President Idi Amin Dada says if that is Captain Gore speaking, the Field Marshal wishes to send his greetings and announces that he is prepared to grant a full and unconditional pardon if you land at Entebbe with your merchandise."

"Well, well, well," said Martin. "Kindly present Captain Gore's compliments to His Majesty Field Marshal President Idi Amin Dada and tell him to go and stuff himself."

There was an almost beatific smile on Martin's face as he said it. Then he became serious again.

"Now Zambia and Malawi, it's up to you. Let's hear what you're prepared to spend on our goodies. We're asking two hundred thousand dollars. What do you say?"

While they were listening for the first of these replies, another voice came loud and clear through their earphones.

"Juliet Mike Oscar, this is Zambia Radio. I have a message for you."

Martin said, "Go ahead."

"Zambia Radio. Message reads, 'Payment by letter of credit only'."

Martin laughed.

"No joy, Zambia old fruit. Looks like Malawi."

They were about to turn when a new voice could be heard faintly.

"This is UNITA. We are expecting those arms. Our lives are in danger. Please follow your instructions. We will arrange a cash payment."

Martin looked at Harry. His co-pilot nodded. So did Stubbles.

Martin said, "Always a sucker for a hard luck story. Sold to UNITA. We're on our way."

*   *   *

The telex was addressed to SOVDEL UNINATIONS, ATTENTION N. ROGOV.

It was handed to Natalia paragraph by paragraph as the telex operator fed the tape into a decoding machine. The first three of these paragraphs informed her graphically of the loss of Uglov and Umboto and the MIG.

The telex continued: IT IS MY CONSIDERED VIEW THAT NO PROPAGANDA VALUE CAN NOW BE OBTAINED FROM THIS OPERATION WHICH MUST BE CONSIDERED A TOTAL FAILURE. YOU ARE INSTRUCTED TO DESTROY ALL DOCUMENTS PERTAINING TO THE TARGET AIRCRAFT AND THE EVIDENCE SUPPLIED TO YOU. YOU ARE TO RETURN TO MOSCOW ON THE FIRST AVAILABLE FLIGHT TOMORROW AND BE PREPARED TO MAKE FULL JUSTIFICATION TO ENQUIRY INSTI-TUTED BY CHIEFS OF AIR STAFF INTO LOSS OF VALUABLE FIGHTER PLANE AND DISTINGUISHED SOVIET OFFICER. ACKNOWLEDGE THIS IMMEDI-ATELY — LITVINOFF.

Natalia read this paragraph several times. The telex opera-tor, an anonymous young Georgian bureaucrat, turned and saw that tears were well into the young woman's eyes.

He could have said something sympathetic. He might even have held out a friendly hand. But he chose to ignore the tears. His was a good posting and he wanted to keep it. He said, quite coldly, "Any reply?"

She turned away from him and looked at a big wall communications map of the world instead, trying to focus her eyes on the African coast where it had happened.

"Ask him what happened to the other aircraft."

The operator typed out the message. They waited for a few seconds and the machine began to chatter furiously.

THE TARGET AIRCRAFT IS NO LONGER OUR CONCERN. FOR YOUR INFORMATION SOVIET NAVAL RADAR INDICATES THAT IT CONTINUED ON COURSE AND PROBABLY REACHED DESTINATION. CONFIRM IMMEDIATELY YOUR RETURN TOMORROW. YOUR RESERVATION CONFIRMED VIA AEROFLOT 216 LEAVING NEW YORK 0920 — LITVINOFF.

Natalia said, "Confirm my return, please. Thank you."

She left the telex room and went into the office which had been prepared for her. Her evidence, together with that prepared for her, was contained in two manilla envelopes.

She sat at the desk and opened one of them and took out an enlarged photograph of Martin Gore. She looked at it for a long time.

She spoke softly in English.

"Oh you bastard," she said. "You clever, devious bastard."

She took a paper handkerchief from her handbag wiped her face and repaired her eye make-up in a hand-mirror.

Then she took the documents along the corridor and placed them one by one into a shredding machine. The last document to be turned into a thousand strips of useless paper was the photograph of Martin Gore.

*   *   *

They plunged on through that star-crazy night, oblivious of the wonderment around them and careless, too, of the anger and hostility which poured through their headsets from controllers on the ground below who demanded their immediate landing and explanations. They heard themselves described to their fellow airmen as a menace to navigation and they heard, too, scheduled flights being diverted well away from their path.

They flew well below the air lanes and maintained a constant radar scan for innocent and friendly flyers as well as hostile fighters.

All three men knew now, finally and irrevocably, that they were driving a rogue aeroplane over a land they did not know to a destination which they might never find. They knew that their flying careers were finished. The exultation of the previous few minutes had turned savagely into a desperate need to be on the ground and away from this screeching coop in the sky and the horror which lay on the bunk so close behind them.

Using the airports at Livingstone and Sesheke as beacons, they entered the Caprivi Strip and began to fly westwards in search of the beacon which Sorrel had told them about. Harry swung the direction finder continually in search of the transmitter. Martin and Stubbles watched the fuel. At this altitude they were burning it far too quickly.

They maintained a constant running equation which centred around a point of return which would allow them to land at least safely in Sesheke even though they were certain to end up in a Zambian prison. With thirty minutes of fuel left they were approaching this very line.

Martin said, "I'm sorry, I seem to have screwed it up for all of you."

Stubbles made a minimal adjustment on the panel above him.

"I dunno, Captain," he said. "Maybe they'll be so delighted with the cargo we bring them that they'll just let us walk away."

"Not a chance," murmured Martin. "The girl's death will

need to be explained. And there's the murder charge from Djibouti, three or four charges of transgressing air-space, misuse and abuse of radio telecommunications and the unlawful importing of weapons. It'll be a show trial — exactly as the Russians wanted."

Harry was half leaning forward, his hands pressing the headset closer to his ears. Martin tapped him, but the co-pilot waved him away irritably. He screwed his face tightly with the effort of concentration and then he turned to Martin.

"Dot . . . dash . . . dot!" he shouted. His face was a colossal smile.

"Dot . . . dash . . . dot!"

"Where?"

"About fifty miles I guess. Straight ahead."

*   *   *

Harry had made a calculated guess that the 'R' beacon was only fifty miles west of the position from which they first heard the faint Morse. He had failed to take into account the cleanness of the night air which gave this low-powered signal a much exaggerated strength and clarity. They had flown well over a hundred miles before they saw a faint, orange-coloured glow directly ahead of them. Martin held their height until they were able to distinguish the light clearly.

"I'll circle once and then we'll go in low," he announced.

"Make it a good tight circle, Captain," said Stubbles. His voice had lost none of its querulous innocence. "As far as the books and the gauges are concerned, we ran out of fuel five minutes back."

"If I could see a strip, I'd go straight in," said Martin. "I just don't see a strip."

"Shall I flash the lights as the girl said?" asked Harry.

"Thanks, Harry." Martin was apologetic. "That's how scrambled your mind gets. I'd forgotten."

Within a few seconds of the giant landing lights flashing out the one letter 'G', the blackness surrounding the big orange beacon was brought to life by the lighting of two parallel rows of fire. They caught a quick glimpse of men running with flaming torches and the lights of waiting trucks below.

Martin banked steeply and they were flying back, the airstrip now fully lit, below and to their left. They completed their landing checks and as they turned again for their final approach, they could see a red smoke flare brilliantly illuminated in the light of a vehicle. The smoke was rising vertically.

Harry said, "That's the crosswind component solved. What about the barometric pressure?"

Martin said, "Forget that. I wouldn't mind a few circles and bumps to find out what the texture of the ground is like."

The strip was a mile ahead. Juliet felt as though she was hovering as they brought her back to the slowest possible landing speed and let her fall easily towards the threshold.

"We leave the motors running," murmured Martin softly. "We leave the landing lights on and we'll turn back facing the runway. Might as well be sure."

"Do you reckon they've got cash?" asked Harry.

"At this stage of the game, I'd take shoelaces," said Martin tersely. "Full flaps."

Stubbles interjected brightly. "Captain, I've been loathe to ask before, but these UNITA characters — are they good guys or bad guys?"

He never heard the answer. As Juliet roared her way towards the lights ahead, a single .303 bullet, fired from the ground below, entered the flight-deck through the thin alloy fabric and tore through the equally vulnerable clothing and skin of the engineer. It killed him instantly as it passed upwards through his left lung, his shoulder, leaving his body momentarily before re-entering through his chin and thus into his brain where it finally lodged.

~ Martin and Harry knew nothing of this as they skilfully brought the Hercules in for her final landing. She touched down gently on hard firm sand and rolled only a few hundred yards before they brought her to a wailing standstill.

They turned her, to be ready for an instant take-off. Even as they did so, they knew that they were wasting their time. Men stood at each of the fifty blazing gasoline cans. They were already dousing them with sand.

Martin checked that the flaps were set at fifty per cent for a fast take-off roll and waited for the engineer to confirm that the electrical panel was in order.

"Stubbles?" he said.

"Look, Martin." Harry's voice was a shocked, throaty whisper.

Martin turned and saw Stubbles sliding left upright in his harness, his mouth wide open and his eyes staring unseeing at the instrument panel above him.

He felt a violent coldness in the very centre of his body and began to convulse with retching. He snapped himself together and shouted to Harry, "Come on, let's go — any place."

"Forget it," said Harry quietly. "Look."

In the brightness of their landing lights, Martin saw two three-ton military trucks racing towards them over the shrub-covered sand on which they had landed. They stopped immediately in front of the Hercules and began to disgorge thirty or so soldiers in yellow and green combat jackets.

"Switch off," said Martin. There was infinite sadness and regret in his voice. "Sorry, Stubbles, they were bad guys."

He looked down at the soldiers who were making the now familar ring around the aircraft. The engines whined slowly down to a standstill.

"Those rifles they're carrying," said Harry urgently. "Those are Kalastikov fours. Those are Russian trucks. That's the Cuban army out there. Holy crap!"

A hatless man, young and arrogant in his stance, left one of the trucks and sauntered slowly towards the silent aircraft

His walk reminded Martin of the blond French captain in Djibouti. He was reminded fleetingly that the girl, too, lay dead behind and instantly the powerful nausea returned.

The lieutenant was carrying a small sub-machine gun slung casually from his shoulder. He lifted it to his hip and fired two quick bursts into the landing lights. Now there was total darkness outside.

"Douse the cabin lights. Quickly."

They heard shouting outside. The language was Spanish.

"What do you reckon?" asked Martin.

"These guys shoot mercenaries," said Harry thoughtfully. "I hate to say it, brother, but just at this moment, our lives are worth little more than the ferrules on my shoelaces."

*   *   *

The Mid-town rush hour had started when Natalia left the UN building and the first chill winds of winter were slicing their way along the avenues of Manhattan. She huddled deep into a Persian lamb coat and after two or three vain attempts to secure a taxi decided to walk the few blocks to her hotel.

The Russian Delegation was traditionally housed in a large, anonymous and modest building in a sleezy quarter close to Time Square. Delegates without diplomatic status were sent to an even less attractive hotel in downtown Brooklyn.

The streets were a solid block of multi-coloured metal and the city was beginning to dance with light, but Natalia saw little of it. She stared ahead of her, ignoring the fashion boutiques of 51st Street, at which she had once happily window-shopped for hours at a time.

Not long ago, whenever she had turned into 5th Avenue, especially at that time of the evening, Natalia had never failed to gasp at the magic of New York, stifling the feeling of disloyalty for her own beloved Moscow as she drank in the sheer size and scale and daring of this never ending vista.

On this evening she saw none of it and allowed herself to be swept along in the impatient crowds of homegoers. It began to rain lightly but she did not hear the soft thud of umbrellas as they opened all around her, nor did she feel the rain as it stung her face.

She turned into 44th Street where there were fewer people. She walked slowly, pausing frequently to look unseeingly at menu boards as she fought to shift the enormous depression which had settled on her.

The idea of an inquiry did not worry her. She could talk, especially to a board of men. She could justify.

So her uncle had defected from her side. She had expected him to. He would have had to. The KGB maintained its invulnerability only because it never admitted its mistakes. She was a scapegoat.

She, N Rogov, was, as they said here in this city, the patsy. There would be punishment, of course. There would be a censure by the Central Committee which would appear in her Party records for the rest of her life; and most likely she would be demoted and probably transferred to some remote steel town in the Urals or maybe to awful diplomatic posting like old Turok in Djibouti.

The overwhelming sadness stemmed from the fact that she had failed to achieve something which had been a private obsession. She thought about the pilot in that Hercules again and again and said aloud, "Where are you now, my enemy?" There was a man looking over her shoulder trying to decipher the menu on the Japanese restaurant board.

"Did you say something, miss?"

"No, I'm sorry," she said, embarrassed.

"Anytime honey," the man said.

She walked away from him at speed and kept walking quickly until she turned into a familiar hotel and went straight to the ladies' room. Five minutes later, groomed and smiling, she entered the small oak-panelled bar. The bartender was a big man with a healthy, ruddy face.

"Hey, look who's here," he said in a loud voice which dominated the small room so that the early Martini drinkers turned and looked at the strikingly beautiful woman who stood at the bar.

"Hi, Miss Rogov," he said. "Long time no see. How are things in the Kremlin?"

Without asking her he mixed a vodka-martini just as she had always enjoyed it.

"And how's my friend Brezhnev?" he asked. "Any chance of a war this year?"

Natalia laughed and settled on a bar stool which had been vacated for her by a departing commuter.

The bartender turned to another group of people. She heard him saying, "No, she's a real Russian, you know. A real commy Russian. From Moscow. Nicest lady you'd ever meet. Used to come here a lot. From the UN, you know."

Yes, she thought, I used to come here a lot. She looked around the bar and saw people glancing at her curiously. She sipped her martini and allowed herself to be engulfed by an unstoppable flood of memory.

*   *   *

Their eyes adjusted quickly to the extreme darkness and they could see the outline of the windshield in front of them and the luminous instruments on the panel. They were in shock and they knew they were in shock. They were paralysed and helpless and felt themselves heavy and lumpen in their seats as they waited for the next move which could only come from the ground outside.

Whoever they were, they were taking their time in making it. Martin and Harry heard a few more shouts and saw the flash of a torch. And then silence.

There was a sudden burst of gunfire from the distance. It appeared to be returned from the ground on the left of them.

There were several such exchanges and then a heavy machine gun opened up from one of the trucks in front of them and they watched streams of red and white tracer bullets cut perfect arcs in the blackness. And then silence again.

"What the hell have we dropped into?" said Martin at last.

"Search me," said Harry very quietly. "Two minutes ago, I would have given my life's blood to be out of this aircraft. Now I reckon we're safest here. It's the arms they want. They're not going to blow them up."

"The Cubans must have hit our people at the last minute."

"So why shoot at us?"

Martin peered out into the gloom. He could see the lorries silhouetted but little else. There was no movement.

"What do we do, walk out?" asked Harry.

"We'd better face it, they'll probably shoot us," mused Martin.

"Perhaps the good guys will counter-attack."

"Then the Cubans will blow us up."

"Oh," said Harry and let it sink in. "Maybe we could make a dash for it now while it's dark."

"You forget, my dear Harry, that you lost two or three pints of blood just about twenty-four hours ago. You couldn't run the length of this flight-deck."

"I guess you may be right. So what do we do?"

"We need to play for time."

Harry said bitterly, "You mean like wait for the Seventh Cavalry?"

"No." Martin unfastened his harness and stood. He turned and lost his balance momentarily in the darkness. He felt his hand touch Stubbles' shoulder and felt the little body shift towards him.

"Oh Christ, what a bloody mess," he said.

He leaned down and unhitched the engineer's harness and then picked the body up from its seat. He carried Stubbles across the deck and laid him on the floor. Then he stood up straight and felt his way to the ice-box and took out the whisky bottle. He took a fierce gulp and handed it across to Harry.

"I feel lousy about the little man," he said. "Do you know, he never complained once, never questioned. He trusted me implicitly. Now I've got him killed. Oh shit, Harry, why did we ever leave Karachi? We should have told the girl to stuff it there and then."

"We needed the money."

"Stubbles didn't."

"He did. He had a seven days option to buy a little garage in the Bronx. He would have flown this journey without wings to get that."

"It still doesn't ease my rotten conscience," said Martin. "I feel bad about the girl, too. She was a prize bitch, I know, but she had her reasons."

"Oh shit, man," said Harry forcefully. "They're dead. Accept that fact. We're alive. Maybe only just alive, but let's get the hell home safely."

"Optimist to the end?"

"Why not? I've got an idea."

He heard Harry leave his seat and step gently over the engineer's body. He heard the catch open on the locker under the bunk and Harry rummaging through the tool kit which Stubbles had kept there. He heard the harsh sound of metal being unscrewed.

"What are you doing?" Martin asked.

"Buying time."

He was about to say, "How?" when they heard the voice from outside. It was shouted through cupped hands. It was friendly and humorous, heavily accented.

"Good morning, Captain Gore," it almost chuckled. "Perhaps you and Captain Black and Mr Sroka and Miss Francis would be good enough to step out of the aeroplane. Don't worry, nobody's going to hurt you. Just keep your hands up."

*   *   *

"The aircraft has been found, Comrade. It landed half an hour ago just inside the Angolan border."

"And the crew?" asked Natalia. She had been summoned urgently to the Russian Legation and watched the telex clatter furiously.

"There is no mention of the crew. Moscow is delighted. This will cause great embarrassment to the reactionaries."

"But why Angola? I'm certain that those arms were destined for Rhodesia. Those men are skilled flyers. They could not possibly make such a mistake."

The message clerk, who smiled now, said, "That is for you to ascertain, Comrade. You are instructed to proceed to Luanda immediately via Zaire and to prepare the evidence for the trial."

*   *   *

"Well go on," said Harry almost impishly. "Don't keep the gentlemen waiting."

He and Martin were standing at the crew door in the pitch blackness. Martin's hand felt for the big internal lever and slid it slowly across.

"What's the game?" he asked. Harry had been working at furious speed without talking.

"I hope to Christ it works. Open the door," he said.

The crew door swung open. They stood framed. They were lit by the harsh whiteness of a powerful torch.

The mocking Spanish voice said, "Welcome, gentlemen. My name is Martinez, Captain in the People's Army of Cuba. You are . . ."

"My name is Gore. You seem to know that already. This is my colleague . . ."

". . . Harold Irving Black." The Cuban chortled with obvious delight at the expression on Harry's face. "Martin Michael Gore and Harold Irving Black."

"Irving?" said Martin bleakly.

"And you'll know that I've got a blue birthmark on my right buttock, three capped teeth and I'm circumcised," said Harry. "You seem to know a hell of a lot."

"We do," said Martinez. "And Miss Francis and Mr Sroka?"

"They are dead. Inside the aircraft. One of your bastards shot our engineer."

"Not us. UNITA built this airstrip earlier. We took it from them. They must have shot at you. We have a very good reason for keeping you alive."

"Our cargo."

"Your cargo will be useful, certainly, Captain Gore. It is you that we seek. Not we exactly. Your description has been circulated to every progressive government in Africa. The KGB want the world to know that you've been naughty boys."

"How?"

"Delivering arms to an illegal organisation within the sovereign territory of Angola and thereby attempting to overthrow a democratically elected government.

"Tomorrow we take you to Luanda, the capital, where you will face trial. So if you will kindly leave the aeroplane, my men will attend to the cargo and the bodies."

Harry's voice was dry.

"I think we'd sooner stay here."

"I think not," said Martinez forcefully. "I think you will climb down and follow me. Otherwise I shall be quite content to shoot at your legs and thighs. We have a doctor in this unit."

Harry held his hand out into the light. He was gripping the red handles of an inspection light clamp. The metal jaws were held apart.

"Shoot me and this spring is released. It will close a circuit which will blow twenty million bucks' worth of missiles and high explosives, you, us, this plane and most of your men to the great Kremlin in the sky."

"Don't be so boring, Captain Black. It is not a time for party jokes."

"Try me."

"What do you hope to gain?" said Martinez. "We have all the cards. We have time, food and water. I don't suppose you have a lot of that in this aircraft. And if you think you are going to take-off, forget it."

The torch shone upwards onto the swing.

There was a sudden burst of firing as Martinez emptied the magazine into the port flap hingeing.

"Gentlemen," said the Cuban calmly. "I know that you have been flying for forty-eight hours or so and that you are tired. I'm tired. We, too, have been travelling at considerable speed since we heard your radio performance and the exchange with UNITA. If you choose to spend the rest of the night in a mortuary, go ahead."

"We'll talk in the morning," said Harry defiantly.

"There won't be much talking," said Martinez. "You will be overpowered and taken to the capital. I shall not expect my men to be particularly gentle. And don't expect help from UNITA. There are only two or three of them left and they'll be scrambling to safety in the darkness right now. Close that door, please. Your aircraft will be adequately guarded against any misguided escape attempts."

The torch flicked out as they slammed the door and locked it.

Later, as they lay on two of the pallets in the cargo hold, passing the whisky bottle to and from each other, Martin said, "Do you know, Harry old chap, I've known you for four years or more and I have to come to the middle of Africa to learn that your middle name is Irving."

*   *   *

The taxi was half-way to Kennedy Airport when Natalia slid open the small hatch in the bullet-proof shield between herself and the driver.

"I've changed my mind," she said. "Do you know where the FBI headquarters are in Manhattan?"

"I'll find them, lady," said the driver. He shrugged his shoulders and made a grossly illegal 'U' turn across the grass verge and headed back into the city.

He began to talk in a booming monotone about nothing she wanted to hear as she sat and watched the suburbs race by.

* * *

But there was no attempt to overpower them that morning. Martin and Harry woke in a rose-hued dawn and silently went forward to the flight-deck. They carried the two bodies to the cargo hold and covered them with canvas sheeting which they ripped from the pallets. Only then did they open the side door, Harry still clutching the metal jaws but feeling more and more half-hearted about the pretence.

"Good morning, gentlement." They saw Martinez for the first time. He was a physically huge man, a negro with laughing eyes, who sat in a canvas chair in the shade under the wing.

"Still playing your ludicrous game, Captain Black?" he said. "Very well, go on playing for a while. In the meantime, I would offer you the opportunity of burying your dead. We have dug two graves for them. My men will attend."

"Thank you," said Martin sincerely. "I appreciate the gesture."

"Common sense in this climate," said Martinez. "After which I would like to start unloading the cargo."

"I'll open the rear doors," said Martin. The bodies are there."

Harry stayed in the aircraft as the bodies were taken out on stretchers and laid on the sand. A medical officer inspected them briefly and a sergeant photographed them from several angles.

"Evidence," said Martinez gently to Martin, who watched sadly as the bodies were wrapped in linen shrouds. "There will be many questions, my friend. I do not envy you."

The bodies were lowered into two simple graves and soldiers shovelled the soft sand over them. Martin wanted to say something aloud but he felt embarrassed and confused with misery. He made a clumsy attempt at the sign of the cross for Stubbles and he mumbled, "Rest in Peace" for the girl, and turned away towards the Hercules.

The airstrip had been set in a wide, lightly shrubbed flay caused in the desert by the flash-floods of centuries. The sand under his feet was hard and firm.

The Cubans had obviously attacked in force. There were six heavy lorries and several half-tracked vehicles, bristling with machine guns, on the perimeter. Two heavy lorries remained immediately in front of Juliet. The other four were lined up behind her, obviously awaiting the cargo.

Martinez touched Martin's arm.

"Come, friend," he said. "It is time to stop the game playing. I don't believe that Captain Black is capable of blowing himself up and I'm losing patience with him. I'm a humane man and I don't like shooting civilians."

Martin was only half listening. He was making rapid calculations based on the scene in front of him. Harry was leaning insolently against the bulkhead of the crew door with the grip in his hand.

"Give me ten minutes with him," Martin told the tall Cuban. "You're right. You have been humane. I'll talk my friend round. We'll take the trial."

"Good," said Martinez. He sounded relieved. "I would like to be loading these weapons soon before it gets too hot."

"If you let me switch on two of the engines, we can get the air-conditioning working and keep the whole damn lot cool," said Martin.

The other man looked at the damaged wing and the two lorries.

"You're not going to get very far," he smiled. "Go ahead. Be my guest. I need a cold beer."

As the two pilots entered the flight-deck, Harry whispered, "I've got an idea. If only we could start the engines . . ."

Martin said, "That's just what we're going to do. You're thinking well, my brother."

"I've unhitched each of the pallets," said Harry. "You'll need to gun her like hell, but I reckon we could lose them . . ."

". . . and drive home," said Martin. "It's a hell of a risk."

"She'll do it. Christ, she's a Hercules."

"Better than a firing squad."

"So?"

"So we roll."

They took their places as though for a normal start.

"Electrical control panel."

Harry leaned back and looked at Stubbles' board.

"Set."

"We don't really need ground control permission."

They watched two Cuban soldiers walk casually between them and the lorries. The pilots were excited now and talked in rapid, staccato voices. Ahead of them, on the other side of the lorries, they saw the flay widen at the end of the improvised runway. There were several big boulders in their path. Martin was already working out the best way of avoiding them.

"ATM and generator."

"As required."

"We'll use inboards only. The outboards are going to hit those lorry hoods."

"Roger."

The engines were screaming hard as Martin brought the pitch controls into play. He gripped the nose wheel steering wheel and waited until the Hercules was almost dragging herself away from the brakes. He could see men running in all directions. The perspex at his side suddenly shattered and bullets ripped into the engine control panel. Then he released the brake.

She leapt forward with a violence which surprised the two pilots and crashed immediately into the two lorries, hurling them aside like puny toys.

As soon as she was free from the fearful scraping of her hull against the metal of the lorries, Martin eased her speed back slightly and then put her up to the very maximum that the two engines could give them.

They felt her rip forward under them as the five cargo pallets slid along their rails and fell, crashing to pieces, on the sand behind them.

Martin's hand gripped the steering wheel with the strength of a steel vice. Harry whooped like a rodeo cowboy as the captain steered the swerving, bucking, bellowing monster off the makeshift runway and raced it towards the boulders.

One of the Cuban scout cars had opened fire from their right and more perspex flew around them as they dodged the first boulder, almost turning the Hercules onto her wing. They were free now, heading for the first bend in the flay at well over a hundred miles an hour, Juliet bouncing now on the uneven ground, floating into the air and crashing back onto her great fat wheels before bouncing again.

No other aircraft could have withstood that punishment for so long, but the Hercules almost revelled in the cruel treatment.

When Martin estimated that they were at least ten miles from the Cubans, he eased back and slowed her. Now she jogged gratefully. Steering became easier. Martin looked at Harry for the first time since they had started to roll. His co-pilot was caked in dust which had been sucked through the rear hatches. He was shaking his head in disbelief.

"Man, man, would you believe?" he kept saying "Would you believe?"

Two miles further on the port engine stopped and Juliet made a gentle ground loop before coming to her final stand-still. Martin stopped the starboard inner engine.

"What sort of checklist have we got for this kind of situation?" he asked the still bemused Harry.

They gathered emergency packs together and filled plastic water containers from the main tank in the galley and they walked out through the rear. They stood on the sand and felt the heat attacking them.

"North for the firing squad or south for the French murder rap?" asked Martin.

"Lead on, Captain," said Harry, the mirth bubbling up within him. "Whichever way, it's going to be a hell of a long walk."

Fifty yards away they turned and saw the Hercules looming in the desert. Her outer propellers were buckled and there were savage gashes along the length of her hull and the bulging wheel housings.

"Poor old dear," said Martin with genuine sadness. "She looks quite pathetic doesn't she?"

They turned away from her and began to walk towards the distant frontier.

✻　　✻　　✻

The letter read :

Dear Comrade Uncle,

I have chosen to defect to the capitalist system because I feel a deep sense of shame at my behaviour. I must tell you now that the reason for my determination to see the capture of the renegade aircraft and its criminal crew was entirely personal.

During the years which I spent in New York on behalf of the Lenin Institute, I came to know Captain Gore and fell entirely in love with him. I tried desperately to avoid such weakness but it was impossible.

Unhappily, it was he who ended the relationship and I realised then that, somehow, I must see him again. I have taken advantage of you and the entire Soviet system to bring him within our orbit. I was prepared to crucify this man — if only to spend a few more minutes in his company. I'm sure you will not understand such pathetic emotional thinking.

Now, quite suddenly, I am faced with the certainty that I shall not only see him again, but that I shall be required to prosecute him and almost certainly see him marched before an Angolan firing squad.

I cannot bring myself to do this and, accordingly, I must reveal the truth of this whole affair to the American authorities in the hope that they will take the necessary measures to save the Americans on the aeroplane and thus save the Briton.

I deeply regret each of my actions and I apologise to you and the leaders of the Soviet Government for whom I have worked for so long and with such success . . .

*   *   *

As they breasted the first of several hillocks, they turned and took one last look at the Hercules.

"Those Cubans are going to be right on our asses," said Harry.

"I don't think so," mused Martin. "They're going to get those weapons together before they get too hot in the sun. Then they'll need to look after the wounded. They know we can't get far. They'll take their time. That man Martinez, he'd think that way. A pity, Harry. I quite liked him."

Martin took a slim, pocket-sized transmitter from his backpack and slowly drew out the aerial to its maximum length.

"Radio detonator," he said. "I hope they haven't found the receiver. I taped it between four mortar shells.

"Look north, Harry. You'll see the biggest bloody fireworks display since the Jubilee." He flicked a tiny switch. "Safety off," he murmured. "Poor bastards."

He pushed a button in the middle of the transmitter and they watched as the distant sky turned orange and then began to blacken. It was several seconds before they staggered in the force of the blast wave.

*   *   *

In Moscow, Litvinoff read the letter once more and placed it in a file marked "ROGOV, N. — IMPROPER RELATIONSHIP WITH CAPTAIN MARTIN GORE, 1973-74".

He placed it on his lap and gazed for a long time into the log fire in his weekend dacha.

"We knew, Comrade niece," he said softly. Then he fed the file, page by page, photograph by photograph, into the flames.

DENIS PITTS

TARGET MANHATTAN

New York City, whipped with the winds of a 70 mile an hour blizzard, lies paralysed by snow and ice. Moored in the Hudson River is a 500,000 ton supertanker, *computerized and programmed to explode in a blast as deadly as the one that destroyed Hiroshima.*

The deadline : 48 hours
The ransom : $130 billion

As George Mahle, leader of a band of Red Indian terrorists, masterminds his deadly operation from a secret hideout in mid-Manhattan, Ben Boyle, newly inaugurated Mayor of the City, desperately musters his scattered forces. While they work round the clock, frantically looking for a breakthrough, Mahle cooly cuts Boyle's deadline by six hours.

'A winner . . . One of the real cliff-hangers of contemporary semi-documentary thriller writing.'   *Irish Times*

CORONET BOOKS

OLIVER JACKS

MAN ON A SHORT LEASH

Todd thought he'd pulled off the best tailing job of his career. But it landed him thirty years in Hull Maximum Security Prison condemned as a traitor, to a living death. He was the victim of an elaborate frame-up – but who had done it, and why?

He'd been reluctant to transfer from C.I.D. to M.I.6 in the first place, but Mullen had persuaded him. Mullen – head of the department; shady, seedy Mullen. Was he behind this? All Todd knew was that he had to get out from behind bars and discover the bastard who'd set him up. Even if he had to pal up with the Russians to do it . . .

'A brilliant, intensely readable thriller.'   *Sunday Mirror*

'The story twists and turns like an eel.'   *Observer*

CORONET BOOKS

PAUL BRYERS

HOLLOW TARGET

A bomb explodes in an oil refinery at Milford Haven. After years of waiting a group of terrorists have at last put their theories into practice. And their first taste of blood leaves them thirsting for more.

Bomb squad Chief Desmond Havelock knows this job is in a class of its own. The anonymity, the expertise point to something special. Before long Havelock finds himself taking a back seat to the combined forces of the United Kingdom in a desperate bid to outwit and overcome this new enemy.

Britain. Nigeria. The United States. Angola. International terrorism is a desperately dangerous game.

'Masterfully clever and suspenseful build up.'
Publishers Weekly

CORONET BOOKS

ALSO AVAILABLE IN CORONET BOOKS

All these books are available at your local bookshop or newsagent, or can be ordered direct from the publisher. Just tick the titles you want and fill in the form below.

Prices and availability subject to change without notice.

CORONET BOOKS, P.O. Box 11, Falmouth, Cornwall.
Please send cheque or postal order, and allow the following for postage and packing:
U.K. – One book 22p plus 10p per copy for each additional book ordered, up to a maximum of 82p.
B.F.P.O. and **Eire** – 22p for the first book plus 10p per copy for the next six books, thereafter 4p per book.
OTHER OVERSEAS CUSTOMERS – 30p for the first book and 10p per copy for each additional book.

Name ....

Address ....

....